## "Would you like to dance?"

Instead of answering, Amira just stepped closer to Marcus. He took her into his embrace. He'd been waiting all day to do this, waiting all day to lean his cheek against hers, breathe in her wonderful perfume and feel her body close to his. They danced together as if they'd been doing it for years. As minutes ticked by, they were hardly aware of one song passing into the next.

Slowly Amira lifted her head and gazed into his eyes. "You gave me a wonderful day today. I'll remember it always."

She was talking as if she'd never see him again. That was what he'd planned. In fact, in the back of his mind, he'd decided he would take her to bed tonight if she was willing and say goodbye in the morning. But now he knew she was too innocent for a one-night stand, and he couldn't do that to her. He also knew that one day of being with her wasn't enough. She'd brought light and sunshine into his life again, and he wasn't ready to give that up....

\* \* \*

*Be sure to catch the next segment in the Crown and Glory series, THE ROYAL TREATMENT by Maureen Child, coming in October 2002 in Silhouette Desire.*

Dear Reader,

Summer is over and it's time to kick back into high gear. Just be sure to treat yourself with a luxuriant read or two (or, hey, all six) from Silhouette Romance. Remember—work hard, play harder!

Although October is officially Breast Cancer Awareness month, we'd like to invite you to start thinking about it now. In a wonderful, uplifting story, a rancher reluctantly agrees to model for a charity calendar to earn money for cancer research. At the back of that book, we've also included a guide for self-exams. Don't miss Cara Colter's must-read *9 Out of 10 Women Can't Be Wrong* (#1615).

Indulge yourself with megapopular author Karen Rose Smith and her CROWN AND GLORY series installment, *Searching for Her Prince* (#1612). A missing heir puts love on the line when he hides his identity from the woman assigned to track him down. The royal, brooding hero in Sandra Paul's stormy *Caught by Surprise* (#1614), the latest in the A TALE OF THE SEA adventure, also has secrets—and intends to make his beautiful captor pay…by making her his wife!

Jesse Colton is a special agent forced to play pretend boyfriend to uncover dangerous truths in the fourth of THE COLTONS: COMANCHE BLOOD spinoff, *The Raven's Assignment* (#1613), by bestselling author Kasey Michaels. And in Cathie Linz's MEN OF HONOR title, *Married to a Marine* (#1616), combat-hardened Justice Wilder had shut himself away from the world—until his ex-wife's younger sister comes knocking.… Finally, in Laurey Bright's tender and true *Life with Riley* (#1617), free-spirited Riley Morrisset may not be the perfect society wife, but she's exactly what her stiff-collared boss needs!

Happy reading—and please keep in touch.

*Mary-Theresa Hussey*

Mary-Theresa Hussey
Senior Editor

Please address questions and book requests to:
Silhouette Reader Service
U.S.: 3010 Walden Ave., P.O. Box 1325, Buffalo, NY 14269
Canadian: P.O. Box 609, Fort Erie, Ont. L2A 5X3

# Searching for Her Prince

## KAREN ROSE SMITH

*SILHOUETTE* *Romance*

Published by Silhouette Books

America's Publisher of Contemporary Romance

Special thanks and acknowledgment are given
to Karen Rose Smith for her contribution
to the CROWN AND GLORY series.

To my editor, Tina Colombo, for her encouragement,
patience and valuable time she so willingly gives.
Thank you.

 SILHOUETTE BOOKS

ISBN 0-373-19612-1

SEARCHING FOR HER PRINCE

Copyright © 2002 by Harlequin Books S.A.

## Books by Karen Rose Smith

**Previously published under the pseudonym Kari Sutherland**

## KAREN ROSE SMITH

is a former teacher and home decorator. Now spinning stories and creating characters keeps her busy. But she also loves listening to music, shopping and sharing with friends, as well as spending time with her son and her husband. Married for thirty years, she and her husband have always called Pennsylvania home. Karen Rose likes to hear from readers. Visit her Web site at www.karenrosesmith.com.

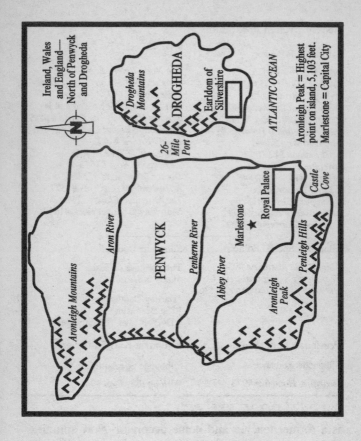

Ireland, Wales and England— North of Penwyck and Drogheda

**N**

**DROGHEDA**

Drogheda Mountains

Earldom of Silvershire

*ATLANTIC OCEAN*

Aronleigh Peak = Highest point on island, 5,103 feet.
Marlestone = Capital City

26-Mile Port

**PENWYCK**

Aron River

Penberne River

Abbey River

Marlestone ★

Royal Palace

Castle Cove

Aronleigh Mountains

Aronleigh Peak

Penleigh Hills

# Chapter One

She couldn't fail the queen. She just couldn't.

As the high-speed elevator dropped ten floors in a matter of seconds, Lady Amira Sierra Corbin felt a bit dizzy. She'd considered this mission from the queen an honor as she'd flown to Chicago from Penwyck. She'd been excited, eager and never entertained a doubt for one moment that she wouldn't be able to meet Marcus Cordello. But for the past three days she'd been thwarted by his secretary.

Monday, she'd been told he was unavailable for two weeks. *No one* could be that busy.

On Tuesday, deciding to be assertive, Amira had confronted his "keeper of the gate" and maintained she would sit in the waiting room until Mr. Cordello had a spare moment.

Apparently, he'd never had a spare moment.

Today Amira had appeared at his secretary's desk early in the morning and hinted that the matter she wanted to discuss with Mr. Cordello was extremely confidential and could change the course of several people's futures. Still the secretary wouldn't budge. But her expression had softened a little as she'd explained that Mr. Cordello had meetings out of the office until Friday, and then he would be leaving the city for a week.

Now Amira glanced around at her fellow passengers on the elevator. She fitted right in, in her violet tailored but feminine suit that was the same color as her eyes. Her shoulder-length, wavy, blond hair was pulled back and arranged at the nape of her neck in a sedate chignon, and her patent leather, high-heeled pumps and handbag were suitable for an early October day in Chicago.

Even thinking about the "windy" city in which she'd landed couldn't distract her from her mission. Where was Marcus Cordello at this moment? Still closeted behind the steel doors to the rear of the secretary's desk? In meetings that would last through the evening and night? Somewhere else in the city where he was making deals and adding to his fortune? All she knew about him was that at twenty-three, he was a multi-millionaire. He owned this hotel and, as she'd so frustratingly discovered in the past few days, he was surrounded by a staff who catered to and protected him.

She had to see him. He might be a prince and the next heir to the throne of Penwyck!

The elevator doors swished open and Amira stepped into the sumptuous hotel lobby with its marble floor, Persian carpets, asymmetrical flower arrangements and groupings of love seats and chairs arranged for tête-á-têtes. It was dinnertime and the reception desk was busy with businessmen checking in for the night.

Her stomach grumbled and she felt a bit woozy as the aroma of steak and garlic drifted from the restaurant in the corner of the lobby. How long had it been since she'd eaten? Not that she couldn't order room service anytime she wanted, but she'd been so nervous about this meeting and frustrated by the waiting that she'd done no more than nibble the past few days. This morning she'd had a pack of crackers and a cup of tea before setting out for Marcus Cordello's office suite on the twentieth floor. Afraid she'd miss her chance to see the man if she went for lunch, she'd sat in the reception area all day, reading the paperback in her purse.

As she approached Interludes, the hotel's finest restaurant, she realized she was starved. Pulling open the heavy glass door seemed to tax her, but it was the crowd of people there that made her realize how extremely tired she was. There were at least ten people milling about, and the bar area was crowded.

As the maître d' looked at her expectantly, her ears began to ring.

"I'd like a table for one." She hoped he could slide her into an empty spot someplace.

"And your name, please?" he asked, picking up his clipboard.

"Amira Corbin. Can you tell me how long a wait I'll have?"

"At least a half hour, maybe forty-five minutes."

Amira didn't think she'd ever felt so hungry or tired in her entire life. Tears pricked in her eyes as she felt a bit woozy again.

She was aware of footsteps and a tall man coming

up behind her, but all she could think about was the wait, or a ride up in that elevator to her room and another wait. Her three days of waiting. Her failure as an emissary of the queen.

The room began to spin as the maître d' gave his attention to the man behind her. "You're early, sir. Your dinner will be ready in a few minutes."

She could barely hear the man's deep voice order, "Don't worry about me. Take care of this lady."

Amira's knees began to buckle as the fuzziness engulfed her.

She felt as if she were floating, then she realized strong arms had lifted her and she was being held against a man's chest—a very broad chest. She heard him say, "I'm taking her to my dining room. Make an announcement and see if there's a doctor in the restaurant."

Being held in his arms and feeling his strength, hers seemed to return. Looking up into very green, mesmerizing eyes, she insisted, "I'm fine. Please don't call a doctor."

"You're *so* fine, you collapsed," he noted wryly. His dark brown hair had a rakishly styled look. His charcoal suit sported a red-and-gray silk tie settled intimately against his gray silk shirt. She didn't think she'd ever seen anyone more handsome.

"I didn't have very much to eat today," she hurried to tell him, not wanting to cause a fuss.

"Then we're going to remedy that." He was already moving with her in his arms. As he strode through the dining room past deep forest-green leather booths, black lacquered tables, and lithographs on the wall, Amira only quickly glimpsed it all.

"Put me down," she murmured, totally embarrassed. "You can't just carry me off."

"I'm not abducting you. I'm taking you to a private dining room. Believe me, you'll get something to eat a lot quicker in there than waiting your turn out front."

"But…" she started. How could she explain about her very proper upbringing and the chaperone who usually accompanied her whenever she was with a man, even though she was twenty years old.

"No buts about it. I've got a porterhouse steak big enough for two on order. You can have my salad to get started. I'm sure there are rolls already on the table."

The idea of immediately having food in front of her made her *but* a thing of the past. This chivalrous gentleman looked totally civilized. Since she'd landed in Chicago, her Penwyck world seemed very far away.

"Well?" he asked, not slowing down one wit. "Are you going to let me treat you to dinner?"

She'd always wanted an adventure. Instinctively she knew sharing dinner with this man could be that. Forgetting propriety for the moment, putting aside everything her mother, the queen's lady-in-waiting, had taught her over the years, she gazed into his eyes and smiled. "Yes. I'll let you treat me to dinner. Are all the men in Chicago as chivalrous as you?"

He gave her an irresistible smile. "Not even close."

Captivated by the beauty of the young woman in his arms, Marcus Cordello could hardly keep his gaze from hers. Her eyes were a rare shade of violet, her hair golden-blond. It looked natural, and from the rich shade of her finely arched brows, he suspected it was. Her oval face was enhanced by the severity of her hair style and softened by her fluffy bangs. As he carried her to the supple green couch in his private dining room, he decided her skin was as flawless as the rest of her, though she did look a bit pale. That concerned him as much as her fainting had.

He asked a question he should have asked three years ago of another woman, a woman who had died because he hadn't been observant...because he'd been too selfishly absorbed in the empire he'd been building. "Do you have a medical condition I should know about?" he asked huskily. "Are you sure I shouldn't call a doctor?"

"No medical condition," she assured him. "I've been a bit anxious the past few days and haven't eaten properly. I only had two crackers and tea this morning."

Gently he lowered her to the couch. "What could a beautiful young woman like you be anxious about?"

"It's a long story," she said with a sigh.

He could see she really was anxious about something, but a good meal would go a long way to making her feel better. "You'll have plenty of time to tell me all about it over dinner."

"Oh, I don't know if I should..."

Just then a waiter came through the door bearing a huge tray. "Goodness, sir. I didn't know you were having company for dinner."

Marcus smiled. "I didn't know I was having company, either, but I am." He glanced at the tray. "That steak's large enough to share, but I'd appreciate it if you could bring an extra helping of the garlic potatoes and the broccoli. More rolls, too.''

As the waiter arranged the food on the table, Marcus took the woman's hand. ''Are you still dizzy?''

''Not dizzy. Just a little…airy.''

He helped her to her feet. ''Come on, let's get some of that food into you. If you aren't feeling better by the time we're finished, I *will* call a doctor.''

Marcus seated the elegant young woman at the table and watched, amused, as she quickly cut her steak and ate half of it along with the potatoes and a roll. By then her cheeks had taken on a healthier pink tint, and he found himself intrigued by *her* as well as her accent. ''Now about that long story you were going to tell me,'' he reminded her after the waiter returned with the extra portions and exited again.

He saw her debate with herself. Then she delicately wiped her lips with her napkin and gave him a smile. ''This is going to sound far-fetched and not something you Americans are at all used to.''

''I take it you're not an American?'' Her accent sounded English, yet not quite English.

''No, I'm not. This is my first trip here. I'm from Penwyck, an island off the coast of Wales.'' She smiled shyly. ''I'm Lady Amira Sierra Corbin. My mother is lady-in-waiting to the Queen of Penwyck.''

If Marcus hadn't already been entranced by this young woman, he might have laughed out loud. She had to be pulling his leg.

His thoughts must have shown in the arch of his brows or the quirk of his mouth because she squared her shoulders and sat up straighter. ''I suppose royalty isn't something Americans understand very well.''

"You're right about that. But I'm intrigued. Continue with your story."

After a few moments hesitation, she leaned back in her chair and relaxed again. "As I said, my mother is lady-in-waiting to the queen. She would do anything for Queen Marissa and so would I. That's why I'm here. Actually my mother might have come herself, but she's on her honeymoon in the Greek Isles and this is a matter that had to be taken care of immediately."

Marcus's amusement faded because of the expression on Lady Amira's face. She was completely serious. Either she was totally deluded or she did have a story to tell. "And what is this serious matter?"

"The queen sent me to meet with Marcus Cordello, the man who owns this hotel and goodness knows how many other businesses. I have something to tell him that could change his life. He might be a prince."

Marcus practically choked on his steak. Finally he set down his fork and managed, "A prince?" How could he not know he might be a prince?

"It's quite complicated. Everything has to do with twins. King Morgan is a twin, you see. But he's taken ill and is in a coma. For now, his twin, Broderick, is running Penwyck. He's always envied his brother, and he did something terrible that he just admitted recently. Long ago he conspired against King Morgan and Queen Marissa and switched the newborn royal twins for a set of American fraternal twins who were going to be adopted by a couple in Illinois. King Morgan and Queen Marissa raised them as their own. At least that's what Broderick says. I'm here to speak to Marcus Cordello because he and his twin might be the true heirs to the throne!"

"You were right about the story sounding far-fetched." Marcus tried to keep his tone even.

"Oh, it's even *more* complicated than that. The queen found out about Broderick's plans before he was able to execute them—at least that's what she believes—and she thinks Dylan and Owen, the sons she raised, are truly the royal heirs. But she also knows that she and the king have been betrayed by enemies more than once, and her plan to foil Broderick might have gone awry. The head of the Royal Intelligence Institute is investigating all of it, but the bottom line is—Owen and Dylan, who have been raised to be the true heirs of Penwyck, might *not* be the true heirs. I need to speak with Mr. Cordello and convince him to tell me where his brother is. DNA tests could settle this whole matter."

Shocked by Amira's story—it sounded like an implausible plot from a soap opera—Marcus took a few moments to think about it while he continued eating. Was Miss Corbin truly acting as an emissary for a royal family? Or was this whole story some ploy to get to him and his money or connections? Was Lady Amira Sierra Corbin for real? And if she was...

The *last* thing in this world he wanted was to be a prince! He liked his life just the way it was. He didn't want to be involved in some royal family's intrigue. Besides, although he and his brother Shane *were* twins, they weren't adopted. His parents might have had their problems, but they never would have kept something like that a secret.

He studied Amira once more. She was beautiful and entertaining, and he hadn't been truly interested in a woman since Rhonda had died. Every time he looked at Amira, his whole body quickened. For the first time in a long while, he was interested in more than the Dow Jones Industrial Average or whether a company was ripe for a takeover. He wanted to check into this woman's background, get to know her a little better, possibly even take her to bed. But he couldn't do any of that if she knew he was Marcus Cordello.

"How long do you intend to stay in the United States?" he asked.

"Until I can meet with this man." She bit her lower lip and said almost to herself, "I *can't* fail the queen." Meeting his gaze again, she went on, "Mr. Cordello's secretary tells me he has meetings out of his office until this weekend and then he'll be gone for a week. I might have to wait until he returns. I have to figure out if it's worthwhile sitting outside his office door any longer, hoping I might catch him. I must think of a better way to get to him."

After taking a sip of water, she set down her glass. "Thank you so much for sharing your dinner with me. I don't even know your name."

The wheels in Marcus's head spun. When he was a boy away at school, he used his middle name, Brent, since there was another boy in his class named Marcus. "My name is Brent," he responded now. Then choosing a last name from thin air, he added, "It's Brent Carpenter."

She held out her hand to him. "It's good to meet you, Brent."

When he enfolded her hand in his, it felt delicate and fragile. Yet he sensed a strength about Amira that intrigued him as much as everything else. The softness of her skin under his made his blood rush faster, and he told himself to slow down. He told himself this was a woman like none he'd ever met. He had the urge to bring her hand to his lips…to do much more than that.

Before he could analyze his attraction to her, the waiter came in, carrying two apple tarts topped with whipped cream. Amira pulled her gaze from his, glanced at the tart and smiled. "Oh, that looks good."

He laughed.

The waiter left as unobtrusively as he'd come in and Marcus breathed a sigh of relief. The staff usually addressed him as "sir" and when he had a guest, they didn't converse with him at all. But there was always a chance someone would call him by name. He found himself liking the idea of becoming Brent Carpenter more and more. He needed a vacation, not only from the city, but from who he was and what he did and everyone's expectations of him. From now on when he was with Amira, he would think of himself as Brent.

As they both sampled their tarts, he asked her, "Have you seen anything of the city?"

"Nothing but the airport," she said with a sigh. "During the taxi ride from the airport to the hotel, I had to hold on to the seat in fear for my life, so I haven't dared take another one. After the warnings the queen gave me about big American cities, I didn't think it was a good idea to go out alone at night."

"Chicago's a wonderful city, Amira. You should see some of it."

"I'm not really here for a vacation."

She'd eaten her tart as delicately as any lady, but her beautifully curved upper lip was smudged with a dot of whipped cream. He couldn't help leaning toward her and sliding his thumb over the spot. Her deep-violet eyes became wider, and her intake of breath at his touch told him she was affected by it. He was, too.

His voice was husky as he explained, ''Whipped cream,'' and brought his thumb to his own lips and licked the sweet topping.

They gazed at each other, lost in the moment. The thrum of sexual awareness between them practically filled the room.

Her cheeks became flushed and her lashes fluttered down as she demurely cast her eyes at what was left of her tart.

''Amira?'' he asked.

She looked up at him once more.

''How old are you?''

''I'm twenty.''

That's what he'd suspected. But he'd also guessed she was a very innocent twenty. Not at all like Rhonda. The familiar pain, guilt and blame rushed in with the remembrance of his fiancée. For two years he'd hardly looked at women. For two years he hadn't wanted the responsibility of a relationship...and he wasn't contemplating a relationship now, he told himself. Amira would be going back to her island. After next week's vacation, he'd be returning to mergers and interest rates and building a new hotel in St. Louis. But for the next few days...

Amira sipped the coffee the waiter had brought with dessert. He'd noticed her load it down with cream and sugar.

As she returned her cup to the saucer, she couldn't stifle a yawn. ''I'm so sorry,'' she said embarrassed. ''I think I'm still adjusting to the time change.''

''Nothing to be sorry for. How are you feeling?''

''Wonderfully satisfied. Everything was delicious." She took her purse from the table where she'd laid it. "You must let me pay for this."

"Nope. It's my treat. You saved me from another dinner alone."

"Do you have dinner alone a lot? Never mind," she said with a flutter of her hand. "That's none of my business."

Her chagrin was enchanting. She was definitely a proper lady. "For a long while now, I've had lots of dinners alone. By choice. I put in a long day and just want peace and quiet in the evening."

"What do you do?"

He didn't want to lie to her, but he didn't know what she knew about Marcus Cordello, either. He answered vaguely, "I work in finance." To forestall her asking any more questions about his work, he laid down his napkin and stood. "I have a meeting in half an hour, but before I leave the hotel, I want to see you safely to your room."

"That's not necessary."

"It's very necessary." He wanted to make sure her lack of food had been her only problem, and she wasn't hiding a more serious condition as Rhonda had.

Amira gave him a smile that made him feel ten feet tall as she acquiesced. "All right. An escort will make me feel as if I'm back home."

"You have a bodyguard?"

"Not as the queen and king do. But when I go out at night I have a chauffeur, and when I attend public functions I have an escort from the Royal Guard."

"Do you feel as if you're always being watched?" he asked, knowing he could never give up his freedom like that.

"I'm used to it, so it doesn't seem out of the ordinary."

A few minutes later Amira was following Brent from the room, feeling as if this dinner had been a milestone in her life. She'd never had dinner alone with a man before. She'd never felt the sizzling attraction she felt toward this man. When his finger had touched her lip...heat had seemed to fill her and she'd been unable to look away from his green eyes. Fantasies had crowded her head and she'd known she shouldn't entertain them.

Yet as the dining room door closed behind them, Brent took her hand and secured it in the crook of his arm. "To keep you steady," he said with a wink.

The fine material of his suit was smooth under her fingers, and she could feel his muscled strength underneath.

When they stepped into the elevator and the doors swooshed shut, intimacy seemed to surround them. She peeked up at Brent and saw he was gazing down at her.

"What floor?" he asked, his voice deep and low.

"Twelve," she answered. Her mouth was suddenly dry, and her heart was beating much too fast.

When the elevator stopped on the twelfth floor, they stepped out onto plush wine carpeting. They passed marble-topped mahogany credenzas, Victorian-style velvet-covered chairs and arrangements created from fresh flowers.

Amira pointed out her room number. "Would you like to come in?" As soon as the words were out of her mouth, she felt flustered, not knowing why she'd asked him. Somehow it had just seemed the polite thing to do!

Brent hesitated. "Just for a few moments." Then he took the key card from her hand and unlocked her door. Opening it, he let her precede him inside. She was close enough to him to smell his cologne, to see the scar on the right side of his brow, to know that being alone with him in her room had been a foolish decision to make.

The small foyer led into a large room with a king-size bed, dresser and chest on one side, and a sitting area with a love seat, chair and entertainment center on the other. A maid had obviously cleaned the room and made the bed, but Amira's pink-and-green-satin nightgown lay folded on the side of the bed so she wouldn't have to look far for it.

Brent's gaze seemed riveted to the satin garment and the king-size bed. "You do know, Amira, it's not a good idea to invite strange men into your room."

"I've never done it before." Her experience with men was indeed limited. At seventeen she'd thought she'd been in love with the gardener, but after an uncomfortable groping session, she'd realized he was only concerned with getting her into bed. That had been her only "intimate" experience with a man.

Now Brent was looking down at her with a flare of heat in his eyes that seemed to consume her. Everything disappeared except Brent Carpenter and the longing inside her. He lowered his head very slowly. Then his lips covered hers and his arms enfolded her in an exciting embrace.

*Swept away.* Now Amira knew what the phrase meant. Nothing but his kiss mattered. The taut heat of him, the trace of his cologne lingering at the end of the day and his musky male scent brought to her mind visions of both of them naked, sharing a bed.

Passion she'd dreamed about, but never known seemed within her reach.

Instinctively her arms moved up to circle his neck, and he pulled her tighter against him. The amazing maleness of his body almost shocked her, but the shock gave way to pure pleasure as his tongue slid along the seam of her lips, coaxing them apart.

She wasn't sure what she was supposed to do, and he seemed to sense that because he murmured, "Open your mouth to me."

She didn't even think of denying his husky command. She wanted to know more about desire, more about becoming a woman, more about Brent. Something inside whispered that this man could teach her everything.

The tantalizing invasion of his tongue sent her senses reeling. Licks of fire seemed to reach deep into the center of her, and she became frightened by it, frightened by her reaction to him. She'd never met a man this sensual or this compelling.

Suddenly her hands were on his chest and she was pushing away. "I can't," she said as she looked up and saw the deep desire intensifying the green of his eyes.

What would he do? Would he be angry? He was in her room. What would her mother think about her daughter having a meal with a stranger and sharing a kiss before she really even knew the man? What would the queen think? Had she put herself in harm's way? Would her life be irrevocably changed?

She stood frozen with the fear of everything that could happen.

Brent must have seen it. "It's okay, Amira. It's

okay," he soothed again. "We both just got carried away."

For the first time in her life she'd followed her instincts without propriety guiding her, and her instincts had been right. Brent wasn't the type of man to force his attentions on a woman. "I...I shouldn't have asked you in. It's not...proper."

A wry smile curved his lips. "Being proper is important to you, isn't it?"

She just nodded and managed to say, "It's the way I was raised."

Although he released her, as if he couldn't help himself, he touched the back of his hand gently to her cheek. "I never met a true lady before." He dropped his hand to his side. "I'd better leave." Then he crossed to the door quickly and opened it.

She stayed where she was, knowing she couldn't chase after him, knowing she couldn't ask him to stay. "Thank you again for dinner."

"My pleasure," he said without smiling, and then he was gone.

After the heavy door closed with a click, Amira ran to it and secured the safety lock, sure that Brent Carpenter considered her the most naive woman he'd ever met...sure that she'd never see him again.

# Chapter Two

Three loud raps on Amira's hotel room door awakened her. Glancing at the clock on the nightstand, she noted it was 8:00 a.m. She'd slept through the night again in a strange place! Maybe she'd left her nightmares in Penwyck. Maybe the news her mother had given her before she'd left—that her father's assassin was dead—had freed her.

There was another rap at the door.

Thinking the maid wanted to clean her room, she slid from the bed, pushed her hair from her eyes and grabbed her robe on the bedside chair. Slipping on the pink-and-green, flowered-satin garment, she quickly belted it.

When she looked out the peephole of the door, she blinked twice. It was Brent! With a room service table.

Opening the door, she couldn't keep from smiling or hide the breathlessness in her voice. "This is a surprise."

His grin was crooked and boyish. "It's a strategic move on my part to make sure you eat more than two crackers and tea. I don't want you fainting into another man's arms."

She knew he was teasing, but there was a serious glint in his green eyes, too. She was about to invite him in when she realized she was wearing her nightgown and robe. "Oh, I can't. I mean—"

Ignoring her reticence, he pushed the table inside. "You don't even have to tip me," he went on as if she hadn't interrupted.

Thoroughly flustered, unable to take her gaze from his broad shoulders, collarless blue shirt and his long jeans-clad legs, she stammered, "I...I have to dress."

Rolling the table to the sitting area, he set the covered platters on the coffee table. "You look fetching as you are. You don't have time to dress. The eggs and bacon will get cold, and don't tell me you don't eat bacon and eggs, because your figure doesn't need watching."

His appraising gaze raked over her, and she blushed to her toes.

With a chuckle he caught her hand and tugged her to the love seat. "Come on. I know you're a proper lady. I won't do anything improper. I promise."

His smile was so beguiling, his manner so offhandedly friendly, she couldn't resist. Missing her family and friends, she felt alone in a foreign land and she enjoyed Brent's company. More than enjoyed it.

Uncovering both their platters, he set the lids aside and settled his gaze on her. For a few moments he simply studied her with such intensity that she couldn't look away.

Finally he admitted, "I couldn't stop thinking about you."

His honest admission mandated she be just as honest. "I couldn't stop thinking about you, either."

He reached up to touch her then, to brush her tousled waves away from her face...

The phone rang.

The sound was a startling intrusion to the beginning of an intimate moment, and Amira really didn't know if she was relieved or perturbed.

"Excuse me," she murmured, and went over to the desk under the window to pick up the receiver. "Hello?"

"Good morning, Amira."

"Good morning, Your Majesty." Amira knew the queen's voice as well as she knew her own mother's.

"I hope I'm not calling too early. I forget about the time difference."

Glancing over at Brent, Amira noticed his surprised expression. Maybe he hadn't really believed she had connections to a royal family. "No, it's not too early. In fact, other mornings I was sitting in Marcus Cordello's reception area by now."

"How's that coming, my dear? Did you manage to meet with him?"

There was no point in beating around the bush. "I would have called you immediately if I had. I'm having a bit of a problem getting to see him. He's very...elusive and protected. I've been camping on his doorstep, but have only seen his staff going in and out. His secretary has informed me he'll be out of the office in meetings the rest of the week and away next week. So I'm afraid this might take longer than we planned."

There was a slight pause. "I see. Well, I know you're doing your best. Cole Everson is working on getting a few more details for you, including a picture of the man. That might help you spot him."

Cole Everson was head of the Royal Intelligence, and Amira knew Queen Marissa counted on him.

"What will you be doing today, Amira? Meeting with Marcus Cordello is important, but you need some time for yourself, too. Have you seen any of the city?"

"No, I haven't."

"It must be very lonely for you in Chicago. Do you want me to find a guide for you?"

Again Amira looked over at Brent. The queen was being so nice, and Amira suddenly felt as if she was doing something very wrong. There was a man in her room whom she hardly knew. She was in her robe. They'd been about to...

Suddenly she wished she weren't on a mission for the queen, and that she hadn't been raised quite so properly.

Marcus had begun thinking of himself as Brent Carpenter as soon as he'd rapped on Amira's door. He hadn't slept much last night, between thinking about her and dreaming about her, though *fantasizing* was probably the better term. The thing was—he felt more than a physical attraction to her. There was something about her that simply fascinated him. Along with rearranging his schedule and canceling today's appointments, he'd called a friend who was an expert at gathering information and asked him to check Amira's background. Now, listening to her phone conversation, he decided she must really be a lady in contact with the queen. This performance couldn't have been put on for his benefit, because she hadn't known he was coming.

He didn't need a dossier to know she was who she said she was and she was looking for *him*. He should leave right now…forget about breakfast, forget about spending the day with her. It would be safer never to see her again…to never let her meet Marcus Cordello. He didn't want his life disrupted again.

It had been disrupted when he and Shane were children and his parents divorced. The divorce had been bitter, and his mother had taken Shane to California while Marcus had stayed in Illinois with his father. They had just settled into that routine, seeing his brother one month every summer, when Marcus's life was turned upside down again because his father remarried. In a way, that was even more disruptive than the divorce because his stepmother insisted Marcus be sent to boarding school. She didn't want to be bothered with him. He'd weathered all of that and weathered it well, turning his interest to the financial markets, researching corporations and how they ran, beginning to invest any money he earned.

Then two years ago, when he'd thought his life was on track, when he'd already become wealthier than he ever dreamed, he lost his fiancée to diabetes. Rhonda had kept her condition from him, and he'd had no idea she was dealing with it. Since she'd died, he'd done nothing but work nineteen or twenty hours a day. He'd cut off all social contact and let his staff deal with the outside world.

But last night Amira had crashed through all the protective layers he'd built around himself, and he wanted to spend more time with her.

He saw her glance at him and also saw the guilty

flush that colored her cheeks. He might have to do some fast talking to get her to spend the day with him.

When she hung up, she looked pensive.

"Is everything all right?" he asked.

"The queen's always so understanding. She's like a second mother to me. She asked me if I want a guide while I'm in Chicago."

"What did you say?" If Amira ended up with someone the queen hired, the guide would surely be a bodyguard, too.

"That I don't."

"You don't want the queen's guide, or you don't want *any* guide? Because I'd be glad to show you a few sights today."

Amira looked uncertain. "Don't you have to work?"

"I haven't taken a day off in far too long. I can't think of a better way to spend it than showing you what I like best about Chicago. What do you say?"

A slow smile crept across her pretty lips. "The queen *did* say I should see some of the sights."

"A royal command if I ever heard one."

At that, Amira laughed and her hesitation seemed to vanish. "I have to shower and get dressed. Should I meet you somewhere?"

He didn't want to crowd her or make her feel uncomfortable. If he did, she'd run in the opposite direction. "I do have a few arrangements to make. Would you like to go to the theater tonight, or dancing at a club?"

"Dancing." She looked like a child who'd been given a Christmas present.

"Okay, dancing it is. Let's eat, and I'll meet you in the lobby in a half hour. Is that enough time?"

Their gazes caught and held.

"Yes, that's enough time," she murmured.

As they finished breakfast, Marcus knew he had to get out of this hotel room, away from Amira and that bed quickly before he kissed her and led her to it. She wasn't that kind of woman, and today he wasn't going to be that kind of man.

Still, she was so alluring, with her blond waves mussed and her flowered satin robe clinging so wonderfully to all her curves. He couldn't keep away from her. Covering the few steps between them, he lifted her chin and pressed a kiss to her lips. It was supposed to be a chaste kiss, a light kiss, but when he lifted his head, he was aroused. It was a good thing they'd be sight-seeing today. If they were on the move, he could restrain the desire to pull her into his arms.

He stepped away. "In a half hour," he reminded her huskily.

Then he left Lady Amira Sierra Corbin feeling more alive than he had in two long years.

The October day couldn't have been more perfect. The sky was blue, the air held a tinge of autumn, the sun gleamed off skyscraper windows. It was a day of play and fun and teasing. Brent found he could very easily rattle Amira with a seductive look, a little bit more than a friendly touch. When she'd appeared in the lobby in a forest-green pantsuit, he'd arched a brow and asked if that was her idea of casual. Very seriously she'd said that it was.

He'd taken her hand, slipped it into the crook of

his arm and said teasingly, "One of these days we'll have to get you into a pair of jeans."

His driver drove them to Wrigley Field. The ivy-covered stadium, one of the oldest in America, seemed to fascinate Amira. From there, Marcus directed his driver to the Shedd Aquarium, the Chicago Historical Society and the Lincoln Park Zoo where Amira was enchanted by the chimpanzees drawing on poster board with crayons.

Somehow throughout the morning, Marcus managed to keep himself from kissing Amira again, though it seemed to be constantly on his mind. He'd never felt this way—not even with Rhonda. Although they'd become engaged, he'd always been eager to get back to work, to hear about an exciting new investment opportunity. Today all he wanted was to be close to Amira, see her eyes come alive with the sights and her mouth break into that beautiful smile. Maybe he was so engrossed with her because he knew their time was limited.

They decided to have ice cream for lunch because they'd had a big breakfast. He discovered Amira's favorite was mint chocolate chip, and as she licked it from the cone, she nearly drove him crazy.

Late in the afternoon he had his driver drop them off along the Magnificent Mile, the stretch of Michigan Avenue created for shoppers. They ended up at Tribune Tower, home of the *Chicago Tribune.* Hungry after that, for food as well as Amira, Marcus took her to a small French café where nobody would know him. Flickering candlelight made her eyes shine with her enjoyment of the day. The intimacy between them caused him to reach across the table and touch her hand more than once.

It was almost 10:00 p.m. when his driver dropped them off at a casual club he'd frequented a few times. It was so crowded they couldn't find a table, and when he led her directly to the dance floor, they seemed to get bumped from every side. Besides that, the music was so loud, they couldn't hear each other.

As the band finally took a break, he held her close and whispered in her ear, "This isn't exactly what I had in mind. I want to talk to you, not shout at you. Would you like to see my penthouse?" He added quickly, "The housekeeper's there so we'll have a chaperone."

Amira seemed to debate with herself, but then she smiled up at him. "I'd love to see it."

At Marcus's building, the doorman opened the door for them. The man started to say, "Good evening, Mr.—"

Marcus cut him off. "Good evening, Charlie. How's your new grandson?"

"Three weeks old today and not a boy handsomer on this earth."

Marcus laughed and guided Amira to the private elevator that led to the penthouse. As soon as they stepped inside, she noted, "I think you live like royalty."

Her words surprised him. "Do you want to run that by me again?"

She listed the reasons why she thought so on her fingers one by one. "You eat in a private dining room. You have a driver. And you have a private elevator. Definitely earmarks of royalty."

He saw that she was teasing him, and he laughed. "I guess some people would look at it that way. But I don't have a dastardly twin ready to step into my shoes." Amira had told him again the whole story about Broderick's hostility toward King Morgan, and he still couldn't get over the idea of someone switching babies with the royal twins. He supposed anything was possible, yet he knew in his gut he and Shane weren't the twins the queen was searching for. They couldn't be.

"Do you have any brothers and sisters?" Amira asked.

"I have a brother." He wasn't about to tell her Shane was a twin. "And he couldn't be more unlike me. He's in construction—a contractor."

The elevator stopped at the top floor. Marcus was glad they'd arrived so he could put an end to the conversation. Family history wasn't a safe subject. She might know more about Marcus Cordello than she'd revealed.

After Marcus unlocked the door to the penthouse, he let Amira precede him inside and tried to see his condo through her eyes. There was chrome and glass and black leather, two original contemporary paintings on the walls as well as a contemporary wall hanging.

Her gaze swept the large sunken living room, the open dining area with its glass-topped table and wrought-iron chandelier. "You're not here much?" she asked perceptively.

"No, I'm not. It's a stopover where I catch a few hours sleep. My office down the hall has a more lived-in quality." He motioned past the living room. "In fact, you'd probably even find candy-bar wrappers on the desk."

He crooked his finger at her. "Come here. This is what I wanted to show you."

On his way to the French doors, he pushed a button on the wall and soft music flowed from unseen speakers. After he opened the doors onto the balcony, he held his hand out to her.

When she joined him outside, the city lay before them—twinkling lights, tall buildings, neon signs. "Now I know why you live here."

There were cushy outdoor chairs on the balcony, and she laid her purse on the table between them and went to stand at the railing. The air was much cooler than it had been during the day, but it felt great after being in the stuffy club.

"I guess we should have gone to the theater instead of the club." He was trying to think about something other than her slightly fuller lower lip, her long eyelashes, her satinlike skin.

Facing him, she murmured, "Then I might not have come here."

The way she said it, he knew she wanted to be here with him.

A slow dreamy melody poured from the speakers, and all he could think about was holding her in his arms. "Would you like to dance?"

Instead of answering, she just stepped closer to him. He took her into his embrace. He'd been waiting all day to do this, waiting all day to lean his cheek against hers, breathe in her wonderful perfume, and feel her body close to his. They danced together as if they'd been doing it for years. Maybe that was because they fitted together so perfectly. Maybe that was because they didn't really care about the music, but rather each other. As minutes ticked by, as the lights of the city below twinkled, they were hardly aware of one song passing into the next. Marcus only knew his heart beat in rhythm with hers, and the heat between them could have warded off the chill if it had been ten below.

Slowly Amira lifted her head and gazed into his eyes. "You gave me a wonderful day today. I'll remember it always."

She was talking as if she'd never see him again. That was what he'd planned. In fact, in the back of his mind, he'd decided he would take her to bed tonight if she was willing and say goodbye in the morning. But now he knew she was too innocent for a one-night stand, and he couldn't do that to her. He also knew that one day of being with her wasn't enough. She'd brought light and sunshine into his life again, and he wasn't ready to give that up.

"You told me you like to jog in the mornings, but you've been afraid to do it here. We could jog in Lincoln Park tomorrow morning if you'd like."

"Don't you have to get back to work?"

"Another day won't hurt. I'm going on a vacation on Sunday, anyway. I'll just start it sooner than I planned. Is eight o'clock too early?"

She shook her head. "Eight will be fine."

And then he couldn't be with her and not kiss her any longer. His hand slid to her neck into her luxurious hair. She'd worn it down today, and it was silky and soft. The style made her look a lot less proper.

As he held her, she tipped her chin up, and he knew she wanted the kiss as much as he did. Where they'd fallen into the first kiss with a ferocity that had stunned them both, he took this one slowly, easing them into it. When his tongue laved her lower lip, she opened her mouth to him. With the lights of the city below and music enfolding them, he felt bowled over by her. He'd never felt that way before. He'd always been the one in control, the one who called the shots. Danger signals went off in his head, but he quieted them with the idea that this could never be serious, that they'd never have the time to get truly involved. Even if they did go to bed together tomorrow or the next day, they both knew that would be the end of it. Their lives were an ocean apart. This was just one of those flings that happened on a weekend or over a holiday.

As he took the kiss deeper, the warning bells kept sounding.

Before his control snapped altogether, he pulled away. "I think I'd better introduce you to my house-keeper." Flora was just what they needed—a chaperone. Besides, he wanted to prove to Amira that he hadn't been lying to her and he *did* have a house-keeper.

*You're lying to her about who you are.*

No, I'm not, he thought quickly. I just haven't told her my real name.

Amira looked as dazed by the kiss as he felt. "That would be a good idea. Then I'd better go."

He saw she felt it, too—the need to be more than friends, the need to do more than kiss. But he wouldn't take advantage of her—not her shyness or her innocence or her proper upbringing.

Taking her hand, he led her inside to a snack of tea and cookies rather than their first night of passion.

Amira was as fascinated by the city as she was everything else about the United States—even more fascinated by Brent running beside her. He was wearing shiny black running shorts. His legs were hair-roughened, his thighs powerfully muscular. His soft black T-shirt was loose. As he ran, it molded to his well-defined muscles, and she could see the power in his body. She was sure he was slowing his pace so she could keep up.

Brent glanced over at her often, and she didn't know if that was because of her hot-pink running suit in the latest fabric for sportswear or because he just wanted to look at her. She knew she'd be a sight at the end of their run. She always was. She'd banded her hair into a ponytail, but strands escaped and floated around her face.

A few joggers passed them as they ran along a wide path. Amira tried to keep her attention on her breathing rather than on Brent and everything she remembered so vividly whenever she looked at him. He'd given her a perfect day yesterday—absolutely perfect. And that kiss last night...

His first kiss had thrilled her *and* scared her. Last night's kiss had opened a doorway and given her a glimpse of the kind of passion they could share. That was almost worse than being scared. It was a temptation from which she knew she had to turn away. Everything she'd been taught, all of her mother's counsel, warned her she was headed for disaster. Yet on this October day, with the sun shining so brightly on her head and in her heart, she couldn't heed the warning.

"Do you hear that?" Brent asked, suddenly stopping.

Caught up in her thoughts, she hadn't heard anything unusual. Now she listened and heard a low whine coming from a copse of bushes. "It sounded like an animal."

"My bet is it's a dog. Come on, let's go look."

Slowly…cautiously…Amira followed.

Pushing away the bushes, Brent hunkered down and looked beneath them. "Hello there, fellow. Are you hurt?"

"What is it?" Amira asked, crouching down herself.

Brent held his hand out to the animal that Amira still couldn't see.

"We're not going to hurt you," Brent said as if he expected the animal to understand. "Can I bring you out here?"

Since the animal stood perfectly still and didn't snarl or bark, Brent gently pulled the dog out into the sunlight.

Amira got her first good look. "Isn't she adorable? What do you think she is?"

The dog was small, brown—the color of hot chocolate—and bedraggled looking, as if she'd been on her own through days of wet and dry weather. Her fur was muddy and there were leaves clinging to it, but she seemed to like the idea of Brent scratching her between the ears. She barked a few times.

Brent ran his hands carefully over the dog's body. "Probably a mutt—looks like part beagle. She's too thin, but other than that, she seems okay. Nothing a good bath wouldn't fix." He examined her neck. "No collar or tags."

"What are we going to do about her?"

"We can't leave her here. She could eventually run into traffic, or someone might hurt her. She needs food and care."

"But if she belongs to someone…"

"In case she has one of those identifying computer

chips under her skin, we'll take her to a vet and get her checked out. Is that okay with you? I know it's going to cut short our jog."

"The jog doesn't matter. We have to take care of her."

The smile Brent gave her almost made her melt. "It looks as though we're both animal lovers."

"Yes, it does." She was finding so many things about Brent that she liked...too many things. Their gazes locked, and the intensity in his eyes should have scared her, but it didn't today.

Suddenly the dog barked again, and Brent laughed. "It seems she wants our attention." He scooped her up into his arms. "Come on, let's see if she has a home."

An hour later a vet had checked the dog over thoroughly and agreed that except for needing a bath, she seemed healthy. There was no computer chip in evidence, and he asked Brent what he was going to do.

"I'll take her home."

"You're going to keep her?" Amira asked, a bit surprised by that, since Brent worked so many hours.

"Just for now. I know of a place she'll be happy. In the meantime, I'll get her cleaned up and fed well."

Back at Brent's penthouse—a half hour later—doggy shampoo in hand, Brent led Amira into his bathroom. It was huge with black and white tiles, a shiny black enamel sink and a huge black whirlpool tub. He filled it while she cooed to the pup and fed her a biscuit they'd gotten from the veterinarian along with other supplies.

"Did you ever have a dog when you were a boy?"

she asked Brent now, as he checked the water to make sure it was the right temperature.

He didn't answer right away, just concentrated on the water flowing into the tub. Finally he said, "No, I didn't," and didn't elaborate. Something in his tone alerted her to pain behind the simple statement.

"You don't talk about yourself easily do you?" Even though they'd spent all day yesterday together, she hadn't learned much about him.

"Usually no one wants to listen," he said jokingly.

Again she caught some truth behind his words. What makes a man bring home a lost dog? Maybe a loneliness in himself? Maybe knowing what it's like to feel abandoned? "I'll listen to whatever you want to tell me," she said softly.

Time ticked by in heartbeats. "I think right now we ought to name the dog," he finally said. "Any ideas?"

She'd learned already that Brent was good at turning attention away from himself, and she let him do it this time. "I think she's the color of hot chocolate."

"How about Cocoa, then?"

"That's perfect!"

Unmindful she'd been given a name, Cocoa put her paws on the edge of the bathtub and peered into the water. Amira glanced at Brent. He wasn't watching Cocoa; he was watching *her*.

His gaze held her hypnotized as his voice lowered and awareness grew between them. "Thanks for being such a good sport about this. It's probably not what you envisioned for today."

With the huskiness in Brent's voice, the sparks of desire in his eyes, she felt breathless, hot and altogether excited. "I'm having fun, and I can't think of anything better to do than rescue a dog."

The crackle of electricity between them was so strong Amira tingled all over from it. Then Cocoa barked and Brent picked up the small dog, depositing her in the water. The pup looked startled for a moment and barked a few more times. Brent casually sprinkled water over her as Amira poured the shampoo into her hand.

A few minutes later, after a sudsing and rinse, Cocoa shook to whip the water from her fur. Amira and Brent laughed and again became caught up in enjoying each other's company. Amira had never before felt a bond like this with a man.

After they dried Cocoa, Brent said, "Let's go see what Flora's cooked up for lunch."

Cocoa wiggled away from Amira's hand and took off down the hall.

"Do you want to let her loose?" she asked, concerned for his obviously expensive furniture.

"Sure. She's clean. There's nothing she can hurt."

"You said you had a home for her. Where?"

As Brent stood and gathered up the wet towels, he was silent for a few moments. "It's a place called Reunion House."

Longing to know more, Amira patiently waited.

"When my brother and I were kids," Brent explained, "our parents divorced. I stayed with my father. My brother went with my mother to another part of the country. Each of us not only lost one of our parents, we lost each other."

"Brent, I'm so sorry."

He shrugged. "We did manage to see each other a month every summer in the house where we were once all together. It's on a lake about an hour and a half from here. Anyway, two years ago I bought the property adjacent to it, renovated the old house and called it Reunion House. It's for foster kids who are separated from their siblings. All they have to do is apply and they can come anytime and spend from a few days up to two weeks together.''

"The project means a lot to you, doesn't it?'' she asked, seeing that it did, hoping he'd tell her more.

"Yes, it does. So does seeing the smiles on those kids' faces when they're together. That's where I'm going for vacation next week.''

His words reminded her they wouldn't be spending any more time together. Brent would be going his way and she'd be…waiting until Marcus Cordello returned from wherever his jet-setting life took him.

Heading out of the bathroom, Brent asked over his shoulder, "Do you want to take Cocoa for a walk after lunch?''

She should end this adventure right now. Her feelings for Brent were growing, and the more time they spent together, the harder it would be to say goodbye. "I should probably be getting back.''

He stopped in the doorway. "Should you?'' His green eyes were intensely dark, intensely questing. Taking her hand, he tugged her toward him and brought it to his lips, kissing her index finger, touching it sensually with his tongue.

Amira almost gasped from the pleasure, and she knew she was going to spend every minute she could with Brent and the consequences be damned.

"Let's have lunch, then take Cocoa for a walk,'' she whispered.

## *Chapter Three*

As Marcus and Amira walked Cocoa, Marcus couldn't imagine having a more enjoyable afternoon. Cocoa did well on a leash, though she often tried to pull ahead. They took turns leading her, their hands brushing as they passed each other the handle. Marcus's state of aroused awareness made the afternoon exciting, but frustrating as well. He wanted to take Amira to bed, yet so many things stopped him, especially the innocence he saw in her beautiful eyes.

Cocoa saw a piece of wind-tossed foil on the sidewalk, jumped, barked and took off after it. Amira ran with her, and Marcus took longer strides to keep up with her. They laughed as Cocoa put her nose in the foil and pushed it.

After they walked at a leisurely pace again, Marcus's elbow rubbed Amira's, and he didn't move away from the contact. "I'm afraid she belongs to someone."

"She does seem leash trained. And she obeys 'sit' commands."

"Someone could really miss her. I think I'll take a picture of her and make up flyers. Fritz could distribute them and put them up on bulletin boards in the area. The pound is already on the alert if someone calls there. I can also notify other veterinarians."

Amira looked up at him with admiration in her eyes. "You're a nice man, Brent Carpenter."

He'd talked with both Flora and Fritz about calling him Brent Carpenter. They were used to doing whatever he wanted and hadn't lifted an eyebrow. He assured himself he had a good reason for keeping up the charade. He wasn't being completely honest with Amira because she was never going to meet Marcus Cordello. He'd make sure of that, because he wanted nothing to do with her whole fantastic story.

As Cocoa led them toward a tree, Marcus asked Amira, "What do you do as a member of royalty? I mean, do you just wander around the palace? Do you plan state events?"

"You must think I have a very useless existence."

He could tell she was half teasing and half serious. "I didn't mean to insult you. I just don't quite understand what it means to be a lady."

"In my case, it doesn't mean much at all. Yes, I live at the palace, but I lead a fairly normal life. I do assist the queen whenever I can, but thanks to her, I'm enrolled in a private academy and earning a degree in landscape design. I need meaningful work to do, too, Brent, just like everyone else. As far as the royal life goes, soon I'm going to move out of the palace and get my own place."

"How will the queen feel about that?"

"I don't know. I haven't discussed it with her. But I need my own life. I'd like to be an ordinary person—no guards, no escorts, no palace. I want to come and go as I please and not have to answer to anyone."

Those might be some of the reasons she wanted her own place, but a sixth sense told him there was more to it. "You don't want to be queen someday?"

She laughed. "Goodness, no. I don't even want to be a princess. Being a royal is not as easy as you might think. There are secrets and state responsibilities and a loyalty to Penwyck that comes before all else. When I marry, I want my marriage to be the most important thing in my life, not second to what the country needs."

That was the real reason she wanted to distance herself from the royal life, he decided. But her mention of marriage and how important it was to her disconcerted him. He'd never seen a marriage that worked. He'd never witnessed two people actually becoming one. He understood everything she'd said, though, and he admired her for knowing what she did and didn't want. Ever since he'd been a teenager, his studies, his investments and work had come first. That's how he envisioned his life. Yet Rhonda's death had taught him that work could blind a man to things he should see. Yesterday and again today with Amira, he found himself completely blocking work from his mind…something he'd never done before.

Cocoa stopped walking, came over to Marcus, looked up at him, then hopped up on two legs putting her paws on his knees. "Does that mean you want me to carry you?" he asked with a wry note.

She barked at him twice.

"That's a definite yes," Amira translated with a smile twitching the corners of her lips.

Scooping the dog up into his arms, Marcus laughed as Cocoa licked his face. Yes, if she had an owner he was going to do his best to locate them. He knew what it felt like to be displaced. He remembered the move from the home on the lake to the city with his father. He remembered the room at boarding school where he'd first found the financial world to keep himself from thinking about the stepmother who didn't want him and the father who didn't want to rock his new marriage. Most of all he remembered the tearing separation from Shane. Yep, he certainly wanted to return Cocoa to a home if she had one.

Home meant different things to different people. His home was still Shady Glenn. Because of the memories there? He couldn't imagine having a palace for a home. Thinking about what Amira had said concerning the life of a princess, Marcus was even more sure he was doing the best thing by keeping his identity a secret.

With Cocoa asking to be carried, Marcus and Amira ended their walk. When they reached his building, Charlie tipped the bill of his hat to Amira and winked at Marcus. He'd also asked the doorman to use his "new" name. Charlie had simply replied, "Whatever you say, sir."

Sometimes Marcus wished his employees would question him, talk back to him, stand up to him. But he'd learned at a young age that having money gave him power.

They took the elevator to the penthouse, and Flora came to greet them as they stepped inside. His housekeeper was in her fifties, a sturdy woman with a congenial smile that touched everyone she met. Her light brown hair was styled in a no-nonsense short cut, and she always wore jade earrings in her ears claiming they brought her luck.

Now she held out four pink message notes to him. "Barbra said these take precedence, sir."

Marcus quickly glanced at Amira. Had she caught the first name of his secretary when she'd sat in his reception area? Apparently not. She was removing Cocoa's leash, totally unconcerned with what Flora had to say to him.

Flora went on, "She said she wouldn't have bothered you, but these are important."

Taking the message sheets, surprised by the reluctance he felt to deal with them—he usually handled his responsibilities with alacrity—he realized he couldn't forget he was Marcus Cordello for very long.

Amira must have heard some of the conversation because she rose to her feet and approached him. "If you have business to take care of, I really should go."

He didn't want her to go, that was the heck of it. He couldn't help thinking of the possibility of having an intimate dinner with her and taking her to bed tonight, teaching her all about passion, slowly kissing her and touching her until he had his fill of her. Maybe then he could put her out of his head. Maybe then he could think about her going back to Penwyck without a sense of loss.

"Why don't you let Flora make you a cup of tea? I'll try to get these calls finished as quickly as I can."

Flora glanced from one to the other. "I baked fresh blueberry scones."

Amira smiled at the older woman. "You know how to tempt a girl. Scones are one of my favorite treats.

The cook at the palace always keeps them in the breadbox for me.''

"It's settled then," Marcus decided. "I'll start a fire in the fireplace. You can have your tea and scones there."

In his mind's eye he could imagine coming home to Amira at night, sitting in front of the fire, telling her everything he'd never told anyone else. That thought unsettled him. He'd never really confided in a woman. Not even Rhonda. He'd always put work first and kept serious thoughts to himself. Is that why Rhonda hadn't confided in him about her diabetes? He blamed himself for her death, and he believed he always would.

Cocoa ran over to the sofa, jumped up and curled in the corner.

Flora cast a wary glance at Marcus. "Do you want her there?"

"She's free to go wherever she wants." The dog's comfort was more important than hairs on the couch.

"I'll remember that," his housekeeper assured him with a smile and then headed for the kitchen. "I'll get that tea started."

Marcus crossed to the fireplace, took out one of the long matches, and touched it to the kindling. The fire leaped up the chimney, and he glanced over his shoulder at Amira who'd curled up beside Cocoa. He couldn't believe how badly he wanted to carry this royal lady to his bedroom.

After one last long look at her, he said, "I'll be back as soon as I can," and strode down the hall to his office.

As he sat at his desk, he told himself Amira was

here today and would be gone tomorrow. That was the reality of it. Just how involved did he want to get?

Two hours later Marcus emerged from his office, his second conference call finally completed. So much for finishing with business quickly. Maybe Amira *had* already left. Rhonda used to get tired of waiting for him and she'd take off to do whatever she wanted to do. They'd been together yet apart, were committed to sharing a life yet hadn't started doing that.

Part of him knew that if Amira *had* left, that would be best. But as he walked into the living room and saw her napping with Cocoa in her lap, he felt the peace and light she brought him return again. He found himself quietly going to the sofa and standing over her, watching the firelight play in her hair, noticing the brush of her lashes against her cheek, the delicate tilt of her nose, her soft, soft skin. She looked so peaceful in sleep. She was such a beautiful woman. Her beauty came from more than her physical appearance. There was a quality about her that was uniquely charming. Maybe it was her kindness... maybe it was her sincerity. Whatever it was, it drew him until he forgot about restraint, forgot about protecting himself from involvement. He bent toward her and gave her a slow, sensual wake-up kiss.

Her eyes fluttered open and she smiled up at him. "Just like in the fairy tales," she said in a dreamy voice.

He knew she referred to Sleeping Beauty being awakened by her prince. Straightening, he said gruffly, "I'm no prince."

He had already proved that. If he hadn't been so self-involved, Rhonda would still be alive. He never wanted to feel responsible for another life again, and he certainly didn't want the responsibility for a whole country. His conference call had reminded him who he was, what he did, and what his life was all about. It certainly wasn't about princes and fairy tales and ladies who thought men on white chargers could transform their worlds.

He was feeling too much for Amira and that was entirely too dangerous. It was time to put an end to this now. "Something's come up and I have to take care of it right away. It's been foolish of me to let responsibilities slide for two days. I hope you understand." His tone was cool, matter-of-fact, not at all personal.

She looked confused by his manner and his tone, and he was sorry about that. He was sorry he'd kissed her again because every one of those kisses were indelibly engraved in his mind. He needed distance from her now. If he had distance, he'd see how unimportant the past two days had been.

"I see," she said softly, transferring the sleeping pup from her lap to the sofa. "I guess I'd better be going then."

When he didn't dissuade her or say anything else, she stood and he could almost see her wrapping her pride around her. "I saved you a scone." She nodded to the dish on the table. "But I suppose it's stale by now. Thank Flora for me, will you?"

"I'll do that." It was killing him to let her leave without a touch or a kiss, but he knew if he touched her or kissed her again, he'd want her to stay. That wouldn't be good for either of them.

She self-consciously brushed back her hair. "I suppose your doorman could hail me a cab."

"There's no need for that. I'll have my driver take you back to your hotel."

"You don't have to—"

"I insist. I'll buzz Fritz and he'll meet you in the lobby in five minutes."

"All right."

There were questions in her eyes he didn't want to answer. There was confusion he couldn't address.

The silence drew long between them until she gave him a tremulous smile. "I had a lovely time yesterday and today. Thank you."

"You're welcome." He wanted to tell her about all the things he'd felt and thought in the past two days, but he couldn't do that. He wasn't used to opening up to anyone, and telling her wouldn't change anything. He was being more curt than he wanted to be, but he didn't know how else to end this, how else to let her know he couldn't see her again.

"It was a pleasure to meet you, Amira. I hope you have a good trip back to Penwyck."

His message must have gotten through loud and clear because her cheeks reddened. "I *will* have a good trip." Then she went to the foyer, picked up her purse and sweater and opened the penthouse door.

As she left, he felt as if he'd lost someone very important to him.

After Amira left, Marcus tried to work but he couldn't concentrate. When Flora came to his door and asked him what he'd like for dinner, he told her a sandwich would be fine. She returned a few minutes later with a turkey sandwich, a cup of coffee and her own special corn-and-pepper chowder. But the food didn't appeal to him any more than the work. Cocoa ate more of the sandwich than he did. He decided walking the dog might help clear his head.

When he took Cocoa outside, the crisp night air was welcome, the sights and sounds of the city as noisy as ever. But as he walked, he kept seeing Amira as she played with Cocoa, as she rewarded her with a dog biscuit, as she'd hugged her close.

As walks go, it was a short one. Twenty minutes later he was back in his apartment again still feeling restless and unsettled and all together out of sorts. Even Cocoa deserted him as she ran to Flora's quarters beyond the kitchen.

Marcus returned to his computer, answering e-mails. There was one from Shane, and he decided a phone call would be a lot more satisfying. He tried his brother's number in California, but no one answered. Shane's life was entirely different from Marcus's. He liked to keep everything plain and simple. He told Marcus he never intended to be rich, he just wanted to be happy. His contracting business kept him busy, and he was more likely to spend an evening in a honky-tonk with friends than in an upscale restaurant with business colleagues. Their lives were so different, yet there was a bond between them that could never be broken.

When Shane didn't answer his phone, Marcus decided that was par for the course today.

The papers on Marcus's desk needed his attention, but after he'd shuffled them around for another half hour, he decided he couldn't sign them. He hadn't read them thoroughly enough.

What had Amira done to him? Cast some spell?

No, that was something out of those fairy tales she

spoke of. She'd simply gotten under his skin and he had to do something about that. A jog would do it.

Checking his watch, he saw it was already nine-thirty. If he ran hard enough and long enough, maybe he could actually get some work done when he returned.

Marcus left his building and took to the streets in turmoil about the past two days, in turmoil about the past two years. Since Rhonda had died, he'd done nothing but work, and it had paid off. At twenty-three he was considered one of the hottest tycoons in the country.

Yet what did that mean?

He could make any deal, turn the tables in negotiations to his benefit, invest in an Initial Public Offering and watch it soar. The last forty-eight hours with Amira, thinking about her, fantasizing about her, seemed to make all the rest pale in comparison. Damn it to blazes, she was a lady and lived on an island across the Atlantic! To complicate matters more, she was looking for *him*, to try to prove he was a prince. He'd been out of his mind to think he could have a fling with her without any repercussions.

Yet when he thought about not seeing her again…

He ran. His sneakers hit the pavement hard as he pounded up and down streets that he knew as well as the back of his hand. He didn't even feel the chill in the air. Concentrating on the impact of each downward thrust of his athletic shoes, he tried to wipe all thoughts from his mind, all guilt from his soul, all feeling from his heart. It hurt too much to have bonds. He'd never had a bond that hadn't been broken in some way. He certainly wasn't going to go seeking an involvement that was surely going to be disastrous.

Yet as he ran, Amira's face appeared before his eyes. He couldn't block it, and he slowed his pace knowing he couldn't run away from his memory of her. All he could do was work and let time pass, then he'd forget.

He'd been running for forty-five minutes. Now he decided to walk to cool down. Still seeing the expression in Amira's eyes as she'd looked up at the Sears Tower, as she tried her first soft pretzel and gotten mustard on her chin, as she'd leaned over the bathtub while Cocoa splashed her with water droplets, he was hardly aware of the man he'd passed lounging in a doorway. Lost in thought, Marcus didn't sense the stranger following him or realize the danger.

Suddenly the mugger was upon him. There was a flash of the blade of a knife. One moment Marcus was walking, the next he was fighting off a mugger, holding his arm up in a defensive move to protect himself from the blade. It missed his neck and went into his shoulder. In spite of the shock of the burning pain, he managed to knee the man in the groin. He felt the knife again, this time in his arm, and he went down on the pavement on one knee.

Then there was a shout. Someone yelled, "Grab him." Marcus didn't know if the voice was talking about him or the mugger.

Everything went fuzzy and gray. He was on the ground. Someone was putting pressure on his shoulder. He was hot and then cold. Finally there was a ringing in his ears that turned into the wail of a siren.

When the phone rang in Amira's hotel room, she glanced at the luminous dial in the darkness. She hadn't been able to sleep. All she could think about was Brent and how he'd dismissed her. What had she done wrong? He'd become so remote...

The phone rang a second time, and Amira wondered who would be calling her at 1:00 a.m. She sat up in bed, suspecting someone had the wrong room. It couldn't be the queen. It would only be 7:00 a.m. in Penwyck. Unless— What if the king's condition had worsened? He'd still been in a coma the last time she'd talked with the queen. What if something had happened to her mother or Harrison?

Fully awake now, she snatched up the receiver and switched on the bedside lamp. "Hello?"

"Lady Amira?"

The voice sounded familiar, but it wasn't the queen or her private secretary.

"It's Flora. Mr....Mr. Carpenter's housekeeper. I know it's terribly late, but I'm worried about Mr. Carpenter."

"What's happened, Flora?"

"He went for a jog tonight and was mugged. The mugger had a knife."

For a moment she remembered the night her father had been killed, the member of the royal guard telling her mother what had happened. She could hardly get her words out past the lump in her throat. "Is Brent all right?"

"That's why I phoned you. He called Fritz to pick him up at the hospital, and he got home about ten minutes ago. He looks terrible. The doctor wanted to keep him overnight, but he insisted they let him come home. I'm not sure what to do."

"What do you need, Flora? What does *he* need?"

"That's just it, Your Ladyship, I don't know. He's closed his office door and says he doesn't want to be bothered. But he should be in bed. He doesn't have anyone here. His father's in Minneapolis. Since he won't let me near him, I thought maybe he'd let *you* help. I thought if you came over, maybe you could talk some sense into him.''

After what had happened this afternoon, Amira didn't think he'd listen to her any better than Flora, but she could give it a try. "I'll get dressed and catch a cab.''

"No need for that, Your Ladyship.''

"It's Amira,'' she said gently. The housekeeper had been impressed with her title ever since Brent had introduced them. But the title was an encumbrance now. She had a feeling her title and her connections to royalty were one of the reasons Brent had backed off.

The housekeeper went on, "I spoke to Fritz about what I was going to do. He'll be on his way to fetch you as soon as I hang up. You shouldn't be out in a cab alone at night.''

"Thank you, Flora. If you think that's best.''

"I do, Your…I mean, Amira. Thank you so much for helping. Mr. C-Carpenter shouldn't be alone right now.''

The housekeeper's words ringing in her ears, her heart pounding, Amira quickly dressed in black flannel slacks and a white pullover sweater. Hurriedly she brushed her hair and pulled it back into a ponytail, clipping it with a gold barrette. She tried not to think about what had happened to Brent tonight. Certainly the doctors wouldn't have let him come home if he was seriously hurt. Yet, on the other hand, she suspected his determination would have convinced any doctor to let him go.

When Amira reached the lobby, the hotel doorman was holding the door for Fritz. The chauffeur had a grim expression on his face. "I'm glad Flora called you, miss."

"I'm glad she did, too. Let's go."

The doorman at Brent's building recognized Amira and tipped his hat to her. Apparently in Chicago everyone came and went at all hours of the night.

Amira stepped into the elevator, beginning to worry about her decision to come here. What if Brent didn't want to talk to her? What if he thought she was meddling?

She *was* meddling, but she cared about him more than she wanted to admit. After the way she'd left tonight, she thought she would never see him again.

Flora was waiting for her and opened the door before Amira could knock. Her brows were creased with worry as she let Amira inside. "He's still in his office. I offered to bring him tea or soup, but he says he doesn't want anything."

Amira dropped her purse and sweater on the foyer chair. "I'll see what I can do." Then she crossed the living room and went down the hall to his office. For a few moments she stood at the door listening. She could hear nothing inside.

She knocked softly.

Brent's gritty voice came from within. "I told you, Flora, I don't need anything." He sounded strained, as if talking was an effort.

Instead of waiting for permission to enter, which he'd probably deny, she opened the door and stepped inside. "It's not Flora, Brent, it's me."

He was seated at his desk and had a glass in his hand. It was half-full of amber liquid. Whiskey, she suspected. He was shirtless, and his left shoulder was swathed in gauze and tape. There was another patch of gauze farther down his arm. His hair was disheveled and his face was ashen.

Staring at her, he asked, "What are *you* doing here?"

# Chapter Four

Amira realized that, in a sense, she was seeing Brent naked. He looked like death warmed over and probably felt like it, too. That's why he'd ordered Flora to go away. He didn't want anyone to see him like this. If he felt vulnerable and weak, he was the type of man who would fight against that and hide it until his last breath.

Afraid for him, caring so deeply that she hurt along with him, she tried to keep her voice light. "I'm making the rounds of businessmen who got mugged tonight. A sixth sense told me you might not be listening to doctor's orders."

He scowled at her. "Sixth sense my foot. If Flora called you, I'll fire her."

His threat lacked conviction, but she still protested, "No, you won't. She did the right thing. She's worried about you, Brent. You should be in a hospital. All she had to do was take one look at you and know that. *I* know that. Why didn't you stay?"

He took a sip of the amber liquid as if to fortify himself before he set down his glass. "They insisted I had to wear a hospital gown. I don't *wear* hospital gowns."

Any other time she was sure she would have seen sparkles of amusement in his eyes with the words. Now he was just trying to make her believe he wasn't as hurt as he was.

He looked at the glass sitting on the desk, then picked it up again and took another swallow. "You didn't tell me why you're here."

"Once Flora told me what happened, I was worried, too."

She approached him slowly, not sure she *did* belong here. Standing at the side of his desk, she saw he was wearing running shoes and red jogging shorts. Wasn't he cold sitting there like that? Then she realized the whiskey was probably making him hot as well as dulling the pain.

She nodded to the glass. "Did the doctor prescribe that?"

"No," he drawled. "He prescribed pills. They might dull the pain, but they make everything else fuzzy, too. I need to be able to think straight."

He needs to be in control, she thought to herself. "What were the doctor's orders?"

He gave her a narrowed glance. "Something about not moving around too much."

"You should at least be in bed."

"I have work to do," he grumbled.

"You can't work in your condition!"

"You have no idea what condition I'm in," he muttered.

"Yes, I do. I can see the lines around your mouth

and on your forehead. They're telling me you're in pain. Your color isn't good, either. And from the size of that gauze patch, I'd say you were hurt more than you want to admit.''

"What were you, a nurse in a previous lifetime?''

She kept telling herself his gruffness was a protective shield. "I might live in a palace, but I'm not a stranger to the human condition. I know you don't want me here, but I think you need me here.''

This time he merely glared at her in stony silence.

"At least let me help you to the sofa.''

"I don't need a nurse.''

"Then consider me a friend.'' Worrying that the heat coming from his body emanated from more than the whisky he'd drunk, she put a hand to his forehead.

He leaned away. "I might not be taking the pain pills, but I *am* on antibiotics. I'm not so foolish as to disregard the possibility of infection. The doctor made sure of that.''

"I'm glad to see you have some common sense,'' she returned. She knew if she didn't stand up to him, she might as well go back to her hotel.

"What happened to the proper, demure lady I had dinner with the other night?''

"She came up against a stubborn male who doesn't know what's good for him.''

His gaze locked on hers, and then he closed his eyes and shook his head in frustration. "Go away, Amira.''

Instead of doing as he commanded, she knelt by his side and covered his hand with hers. "What are you going to accomplish by trying to make yourself work tonight? If you rest, if you give your body what it needs, you'll get better faster.'' She motioned to the glass. "Or have you already drunk too much of that to see reason?"

Silent for a very long time, he finally responded, "This is my first glass, and I haven't even had half of it."

"Will you let me help you to the sofa?" she prodded gently.

"There's nothing wrong with my legs. It's my shoulder that feels as if it has a branding iron on it."

Rising to her feet, she stood, watching him expectantly.

When he pushed himself up from the desk, he winced. She imagined any movement would hurt right now. Avoiding her gaze, he moved slowly over to the leather sofa.

Before he got there, she hurried ahead of him, propping a pillow against the arm.

He gave her a long look, then sank down heavily onto the camel leather.

"I'm going to get you something to drink. Would you like anything to eat?"

"I don't need anything—"

"Liquids will help you heal."

"All right," he gave in with a sigh.

Before he could change his mind, she hurried to the kitchen.

Flora had already boiled water for tea and had a tray ready with apple juice and a scone.

After Flora poured the tea, Amira picked up the tray. "I need a cover for him, too."

"I'm just glad he's listening to you."

"I'm being persistent about it. At least if he lets me watch over him and he needs further medical attention, we can call Emergency Services."

"I hope that's not necessary. He'd hate that."

"I know he would."

The two women exchanged a look that said they knew the man better than he thought they did.

Flora hurried ahead of Amira. When Amira was at Brent's door, the housekeeper handed her a light blanket.

"Thanks, Flora. Why don't you go to bed. If I need anything, I promise I'll come get you."

"Are you sure? I'll be glad to stay up."

"I'm sure. Where's Cocoa?" She'd forgotten all about the dog in the commotion.

Flora smiled. "Curled up at the bottom of my bed. She's been asleep for a while now."

"I'm hoping Brent will sleep, too. That will be the best thing for him."

The housekeeper nodded and headed for her suite on the other side of the kitchen.

Pushing the door open, Amira entered Brent's office again and set the tray on the desk. Glancing at him, she saw that his eyes were closed. With a shake of her hand, she unfolded the blanket and covered him with it. Then she unlaced his sneakers and pulled them off, one by one.

When she was finished, he looked up at her. "Why did you come?"

She decided to tell him the blatant truth. "Because I care about you."

"Don't," he rasped.

"Caring is just something that happens," she said simply as she pulled a chair close to the sofa and offered him the glass of apple juice.

He didn't take it, but instead gestured to the chair. "What are you doing?"

"I'm going to watch over you for a while. I told Flora to go to bed. She needs her sleep."

"And you don't?"

"Would you rather have the tea?" she asked sweetly when he didn't take the glass of apple juice.

"Juice is fine," he said with a dark look.

While he drank, she sat down beside him.

After he finished it, she took the glass from him and set it on the floor next to her chair. "Did they catch the man who did this?"

"Yes."

She reached out and touched his arm. "Brent, I'm so sorry this happened to you." And she was so very grateful his injuries hadn't been worse. She'd never forgotten the look on her mother's face the night she'd been told her husband was dead. Amira knew it wasn't the same at all because she'd only known Brent a short time, but she would have known terrible anguish, too, if his wounds had been fatal.

Brent gazed at her, the expression in his green eyes undecipherable. But then, as if he could no longer put up resistance, he covered her hand on his arm with his. "You're a special woman, Amira."

"Not so special. Anyone could bring you juice and tea."

"I wouldn't let just anyone be in here right now."

She knew that was true.

When he closed his eyes, she didn't know if it was because of the pain or because he was tired. "Try to rest," she said softly.

"You can't sit there all night," he mumbled, eyes still closed.

"I'll sit here until you fall asleep."

His fingers remained covering her hand as if he

needed the contact with her, but she felt the pressure ease a bit as he seemed to relax. "Thank you, Amira," he said huskily.

She didn't want his thanks. She impossibly wanted a whole lot more.

The first rays of light streamed in the office windows when Amira awakened the next morning. Brent had stirred and she was concerned he needed something. As she'd sat beside him last night, making sure he was asleep, she'd been so tempted to brush his hair from his brow and put her lips to his cheek. But she didn't feel the freedom to take such intimacies. What would he think of her if he'd awakened? So she'd satisfied herself with watching him, making sure his chest rose and fell with deep, even breaths. Only when she couldn't keep her eyes open a moment longer had she tucked herself into the corner of the sofa by his feet.

The weight in her lap made her smile. Sometime during the night, she'd heard Cocoa's paws on the parquet floor right before she jumped up and settled down with her. It had been comforting to have her there, keeping watch, too.

Now Amira's gaze met Brent's in the early-morning shadows. "Good morning," she said, her voice still fuzzy from sleep.

She was grateful that Brent's color looked better. His dark beard stubbled his chin, and he looked roguish and altogether too sexy. She suspected any bruises he'd gotten in the scuffle last night would make themselves even more known today.

When he hiked himself up against the pillow at the

arm of the sofa, he grimaced. She could almost feel his discomfort.

"Have you been here all night?" he asked.

"Yes. You didn't think I'd leave and take the chance you'd get up in the middle of the night and work did you?"

At that he almost smiled as he nodded to Cocoa. "I see you even brought in reinforcements."

Relieved his sense of humor was back in place this morning, proving he felt a little better, she said honestly, "I wanted to be here in case you needed something."

Cocoa sat up in her lap, jumped down to the floor and went over to stand beside Brent. When Brent leaned down and rubbed his hand over the dog's head, Cocoa put her paws on the sofa and licked Brent's face. That greeting and measure of comfort finished, she trotted over to the rug by the bookshelves and settled in front of them.

Brent's green eyes were intense as they returned to Amira's. "I still can't believe you came last night."

"Why can't you believe it?"

"Because we've only known each other a few days."

"It feels as if it's been longer than a few days," she mused. "Besides, Flora said you needed me. Not many people in my life have needed me." She sat up and swung her legs to the floor.

Brent hiked himself up further and tossed the blanket aside. She could still feel his gaze on her as he asked, "Have you ever been seriously involved with a man?"

"No, not seriously...though when I was seventeen I thought I was in love with someone."

"Someone at the palace?"

She knew he was thinking about the royal family, about the Royal Guard, about other men her mother or the queen might have deemed worthy for her. "He was the gardener. I remember the day I stopped to talk to him. I hadn't even been out on a date at that point. He was clipping the hedges, and he gave me one of those looks men give women when they want to stop them from walking by."

"You were seventeen and hadn't been out on a date?" Brent asked, astonished.

"Whenever I needed an escort to a royal function, the queen chose one of the Royal Guards to accompany me. Sean was so different from any of them. He wasn't stilted or formal. He acted as if he wanted to be with me."

"How old was he?"

"Twenty-four."

Brent grunted. "Old enough to know he shouldn't be fooling around with someone as young as seventeen."

"I didn't realize that then. I didn't realize the flirting and the compliments didn't mean anything to him. After I met him a few times in one of the gardens, he kissed me and tried...more. I figured out what he really wanted was to get me into bed, maybe so he could brag about it. When I rejected his advances, he got nasty and said I'd better grow up, that I'd better learn how to give men what they wanted or I'd be a very *lonely* lady for the rest of my life."

Brent muttered a curse, and she looked up at him, surprised.

"I'm not much better than that gardener," he admitted, his brows furrowed. "That first evening I met you all I thought about was getting you into bed."

The glimpses of desire she'd caught in his eyes had thrilled her. Now, having him admit the strong attraction he'd felt, too, her mouth went dry. Finally she managed, "You're the most honest man I've ever met."

Shifting against the sofa arm, he looked uncomfortable. "There's something I need to tell you."

She waited.

His gaze studied her for a very long time. Then releasing a pent-up breath, he decided. "Never mind. It's not important. I have to get a shower." Rubbing his hand over his beard, he added, "And a shave."

"You can't get your shoulder wet." She didn't know if he could make it to his room on his own steam, let alone take a shower.

Swinging his legs to the floor, he sat there for a few moments. "I'm still in my running gear, and I smell like sweat and antiseptic. I have to change the dressing on my wounds, too."

"You might need help with that."

"Are you going to help me with my shower, too?" he asked wickedly.

As if she answered questions like that on a daily basis, she shrugged nonchalantly. "That depends. Do you really need help or are you just trying to make me feel uncomfortable?"

Dropping his head into his hands, he thrust his fingers through his hair.

Amira wished she could do the same thing with her fingers. When he'd kissed her, she'd slipped her hand into the hair at the nape of his neck. It had seemed such an intimate gesture that she hadn't realized what she was doing at the time. Now she consciously wanted to do it.

"I don't know what I'm trying to do," Brent muttered. "My shoulder hurts and my pride took a beating. I can't believe I wasn't listening last night, wasn't watching out. I can't believe I couldn't stop him before he did this."

Sliding closer to him, her knee grazed his. "I can only imagine how frustrated you must feel, but it could have happened to anyone."

He glanced at her sideways. "That doesn't make me feel better."

"What would make you feel better?"

When his gaze locked to hers, she could see the desire in his eyes as well as a deep need maybe even he didn't know was there. "You don't want to know."

"Yes, I do."

"Don't tempt me, Amira, or I'll be just as brash as that gardener."

"You couldn't be."

He shook his head again. "You give me too much credit."

"Maybe you don't give yourself enough."

The atmosphere in the room crackled with the attraction they both felt as well as the memory of their kisses. The silence stretched too long, and she broke it. "I want to help you any way I can."

"You're asking for trouble. Men don't like to accept help from a woman. It makes them grouchy."

Laughing, she stood. "I'm not going to retreat just because you're grouchy. What would that say about my character?"

"It would say you're not a glutton for punishment." At that he stood, too, and when he did, his color faded.

"Brent?"

"I'm okay. I need to do this on my own."

"All right. But I'll follow you to your room. I think you really ought to eat breakfast before you attempt this."

"Maybe you're right. I'll make a stop in the kitchen and let Flora feed me."

"I could bring your breakfast in here."

"I'm not going to act like an invalid. It's not in me. You're welcome to join me for breakfast if you want," he said with a wink. "Come on, Cocoa. Let's see if Flora's up."

Then Brent strode from his office as if he hadn't been injured at all. His denial of his condition made Amira watchful as she followed him and Cocoa to the kitchen.

Flora was indeed up and already making breakfast. She took a look at Brent, though, and shook her head. "You should be in bed, sir."

The walk from his office seemed to have tired Brent out, and he sank heavily into a chair at the table. "Once I eat your French toast and hash browns, I'll feel like new."

Amira couldn't help but roll her eyes. "You'll have to patent that recipe, Flora. Every restaurant in the country will want it."

Brent just scowled at her, and she imagined even that took energy. He didn't argue when she crossed to the counter and poured coffee for him.

Fifteen minutes later he'd only finished half of everything on his plate. He was looking gray again, and she suspected this little excursion had tired him out.

As she pushed her coffee cup away from her, she advised, "Maybe you should rest for a while now."

Ignoring her concern, he pushed himself up from the table. "I told you—I'm going to get a shower."

She was determined to take care of him, even though he was determined to take care of himself. "All right. While you get your shower, I'll stand outside the door in case you need me."

"That's not necessary," he argued.

"It might not be necessary, but I think it would be a good precaution. I've had first-aid classes. I can change the bandages for you when you're finished."

His gaze caught and held hers. Then he headed for his room, not checking to see if she followed.

Brent could access his bathroom from inside his bedroom or from the hallway outside. While the shower ran, Amira stood in the hall, waiting to see if he needed help. He'd held his shoulder and arm stiffly this morning, but he'd seemed steady on his feet. It was obvious he was a proud man who didn't want to turn to anyone for help. That didn't mean he didn't *need* help.

When the shower stopped running, Amira listened for sounds of movement inside the bathroom. Ten minutes later Brent opened the door and faced her squarely. He was as pale as he'd looked last night, and he was holding on to the doorjamb. The pair of black flannel jogging shorts he wore now rode low on his hips. Her gaze passed up the length of all that tanned skin. His hair was still damp, and his creased brow and the expression in his eyes told her he was in pain.

How long could he stand there without leaning on her?

She ran her fingers over the edges of the shoulder bandage. It was dry. Somehow he'd managed to keep his shoulder and arm clear of the water. Her fingers not only touched the gauze but briefly grazed his skin, and the steamy atmosphere around them seemed to become electrified.

"I hate to ask you to do this, but I don't think I can handle changing the shoulder bandage on my own."

"Let's do it in your bedroom," she said softly, knowing asking for help was difficult for him. She knew he'd be more comfortable in his bed and by the time they'd finished he might need to lie down.

Amira saw the bandaging supplies on the sink.

"Everything's there that I need," he said gruffly. "The nurse got all of it for me from the hospital pharmacy."

He was standing in the doorway, and there was just enough room to slip past him to the sink. When she did, her breasts grazed his arm. Neither could ignore the jolt of awareness.

"I'll wait in the bedroom," he told her.

Amira quickly gathered up the supplies and followed him into his room. It was decorated in tan and navy and was as masculine as he was. The oak bed was definitely king-size. It was covered with a navy, tan and white geometrically designed quilt. The same fabric draped the windows. A triple dresser was empty except for a wooden valet that held Brent's wallet and change. With the door to the armoire standing open, she guessed his jogging shorts had come from one of the drawers.

"Sit there." She motioned to the edge of the bed. As he did, she realized there was only one way to get to his shoulder easily. She had to stand between his legs. He must have realized that the same time she did because he moved his thighs wider apart. When she stepped into the space, her heart was thudding so hard she could barely hear herself think. Then she concentrated on what she was doing and Brent's well-being...not the exciting, ferocious, scary feelings he stirred up in her.

When she removed the bandage from Brent's shoulder, she saw that the wound was long and deep. He glanced at her to see if she could handle the task, but she kept her mind focused and didn't meet his eyes. She worked quickly for her benefit as well as his.

After she'd finished, he was whiter than before and she knew he'd have to give in to the pain and the need to rest soon. "Would taking a pain pill be so terrible?" she asked.

"I'd rather feel the pain and know what's happening to me. Besides, looking at you is all the pain medication I need."

Along with his discomfort, she saw the passionate sparks in his eyes. What if he gave in to them? What if *she* gave in to them?

Emboldened by everything that had passed between them, by her night on the couch watching him and listening for his breathing, she asked, "If that's true, then why did you send me away yesterday?"

She was standing so close to him, she could smell the soap he'd used, see the line of his beard stubble even though he'd shaved, feel the heat from his body. They weren't even touching and she was trembling all over. They didn't have to be touching for her to feel the sizzle between them.

Brent let out a sigh. "I think you know the answer to that, Amira. If we keep seeing each other, one or both of us is going to get hurt."

Although she didn't want to believe it, she knew he was right. She knew if she stayed, they'd get closer and closer. Obviously, Brent didn't want that. Then she thought about their kisses, saw longing in his eyes now. Even if he did want to be with her, even if he let her into his life, what would happen when she had to go back to Penwyck? His work was here, his life was here. If they *did* become involved, they wouldn't be able to have anything more than a fling because of who he was and who she was. She'd never had a fling, and she didn't think she ever would. Her dreams were about a husband and marriage and children. A girl didn't get those by giving in to an attraction that was too hot to handle.

She thought about everything she'd done since she'd met Brent. She hardly knew him and she was standing in his bedroom thinking about what they'd do in his bed! What had happened to the values her mother had taught her?

Whenever she was around Brent, there was no black or white. There was only gray and the feelings that were deepening for him. She had to be true to who she was. She couldn't disappoint her mother or the queen.

"You're right," she responded in answer to what he'd said. "We would get hurt."

Quickly she stepped away from him and picked up the gauze, tape and scissors. "After I put these in the bathroom, I'm going to leave. I'll tell Flora you're resting. If you need anything else, I'm sure she can get it for you."

He didn't look surprised or disappointed, and he didn't ask her to stay. "Thank you, Amira...for everything you've done. I'll never forget it."

"I'll never forget you," she whispered, tears coming to her eyes.

Then she turned away from him and left his bedroom, before she crawled into that bed beside him and gave him any comfort he wanted.

# Chapter Five

Empty.

Since Amira had left the penthouse a few minutes ago, he'd felt empty.

It was a feeling Marcus had never had before and one he didn't like. Being the man of action that he was, even in his present condition, there was only one thing to do.

Fill the void.

Picking up the phone on his bedside table, he decided Shane should be up. In fact, he might already be at a construction site. Marcus kept telling his twin he should get a cell phone, but his brother just wasn't that type.

Shane answered on the first ring. "About time I hear from you," he chided. "Did you buy the State of California yet?"

Marcus laughed. There was no jealousy between them. Shane did his thing and Marcus did his. They supported each other, happy in each other's successes, sympathetic at each other's losses.

"Not yet. Do you have a few minutes?"

"I should have been out the door a half hour ago. But I always have time for you. What's up?"

Marcus knew how the business clock ticked. If Shane said he should be on the job, then he should be. Marcus didn't want to have a rushed conversation about Amira's story. But he did have a question.

"Tell me something. Do you remember Mother or Dad telling any stories about labor and delivery?"

"Ours, you mean?"

"Yes, ours," Marcus responded patiently. "You've been around Mother more than I have. Did she ever talk about it?"

"Not that I can recall. Why?"

Why, indeed. Even a long phone conversation wouldn't handle this. He needed to talk to Shane in person. They hadn't seen each other for a while... "What does your schedule look like for the next few weeks?"

"I'll be starting a new project. Long days, short nights. You know the drill. Why?"

"I thought I might fly out. There's something I want to discuss with you."

"So discuss. You're asking odd questions."

"I know. I met a woman who started me thinking about some things. That's all."

"A woman? A pretty woman?" There was amusement and hope in Shane's voice.

"Yes, a very pretty woman. But she's not from the U.S. and she's leaving soon. I've decided it's better if I don't see her again. I was going to have Fritz drive me up to Shady Glenn today, but..."

Something in Marcus's voice must have alerted Shane that something was wrong. "You're not leaving today?"

"I was mugged last night."

"You mean your wallet was stolen?"

"Not as simple as that. The mugger had a knife."

"Blue blazes, Marcus! Are you all right?"

"If I don't move too fast. He got my shoulder. I should feel a lot better by tomorrow. Today I'm just a bit wiped out."

"You went to a doctor, I hope."

"I didn't have any choice. Somebody called an ambulance. But I came home last night. I couldn't stay in that place. You know how I feel about hospitals." After Rhonda had slipped into a coma, he'd sat by her bedside for two days. Then he'd lost her. Shane knew that.

"Yeah, I know how you feel about them. At least Flora was there to look after you. Wasn't she?"

"I wouldn't let Flora look after me so she called in reinforcements."

"Fritz?"

Marcus laughed. "He was in on it. She called Amira—the woman I told you about—and he drove her over."

"And just what does this Amira look like?"

"Blond hair, violet eyes."

"And..." Shane probed.

"And she's as innocent as an angel. Not like any twenty-year-old I've ever met. She's been protected and chaperoned all her life."

"Uh-oh. It sounds like more than a little interest there."

"It's impossible," Marcus said in frustration. "She lives on an island an ocean away."

"Are you sure you're not going to see her again?" Shane asked.

"It's not a good idea."

"Good idea or not, it sounds as if maybe you should." There was a lengthy pause before Shane asked, "Is she in your dreams?"

Marcus knew what his brother meant. "Yes."

"Is she in your thoughts when you're awake, too?"

He didn't answer that one.

"You might have to see her again to get her out of your system."

Marcus knew his brother might be right. "She's something else, Shane. She really is. Like no woman I've ever met. I can forget about deals and investments and whether she's with me because of who I am and what I have."

"Then see her again."

Marcus heard a loud male voice calling for Shane.

His brother said, "Uh-oh. One of my subcontractors is at the door. Must be an emergency. Do you want to talk later?"

"I'll phone you next week. We'll see if we can coordinate our schedules."

"Sure thing. You can always help me dig a footer."

Marcus could hear the grin in his twin's voice.

After Marcus hung up, he thought about what Shane had said about seeing Amira again. Should he take the risk?

For the rest of Saturday, long into the night and all day Sunday, Marcus thought about Amira—how special she was, how much he liked being with her, how much he wanted her. She was alone in Chicago, and he was the only person she really knew. If he went away, he'd feel as if he was deserting her.

He wasn't just going to Shady Glenn for a vacation, but to spend some time at Reunion House. He liked being with the kids and making repairs on the old house. It gave him a different kind of satisfaction from the usual work he did, the kind of satisfaction Shane had all the time, he imagined—working with his hands, building. Marcus suspected that Amira would like Reunion House and enjoy meeting the kids there. Yet, after the way they'd left things yesterday, he didn't know if she'd accept his invitation. His father would be at Shady Glenn, so having a chaperone wouldn't be a problem.

But he needed an enticing way to ask her to join him.

Cocoa ran into his office then, barked at him and stood on her hind legs.

Marcus smiled. He did have an idea, and one he suspected would work very well.

On Monday morning Amira was debating how she would spend the day. She'd dressed in a blue, tailored pantsuit ready to go sight-seeing. Yet the thought of doing it without Brent didn't seem very satisfying. She knew she had to stop pining for him. She knew she had to forget about him. It was very hard, especially when she had a week on her hands that she didn't know what to do with.

The knock on her door was unexpected. Crossing to it, she looked out the peephole and saw a yellow wagon with Cocoa sitting in it!

Opening the door, she didn't know what to expect. There was Brent standing two feet from the wagon, grinning at her.

"What are you doing here?"

He nodded to the wagon and the envelope propped beside Cocoa. "Read it," he suggested.

Stooping down, she patted the dog on the head and ruffled her ears. Then she picked up the envelope and opened it, her heart racing. The invitation inside read, "Come along with me to see Shady Glenn and Reunion House. Cocoa."

She looked up at Brent, confused.

Taking the handle of the wagon, he pulled it inside. When he straightened, his hand went to his shoulder and she could tell he was still in pain.

"What are you doing up and out?" she asked, concerned.

With a shrug he smiled. "I have things to do, places to go, people to see."

"You need a keeper," she muttered.

"How would you like to be my keeper for a few days?" His green eyes said the invitation was a serious one.

She didn't know how or what to respond to that.

"I'm going to Shady Glenn to recuperate until next weekend. I know how you worry about chaperones. My father's going to fly in this evening. So he'll be there. While you're there, you can check out Reunion House. The kids love visitors and you can help me present Cocoa to them."

The whole idea seemed like another wonderful adventure. Did she dare go with him?

His smile fading, he leaned toward her, slowly combed his fingers through her hair and smoothed his thumb over the side of her cheek. "Amira, I know we live in different worlds and all we'll ever have is this week. But having it could be better than not having it. Don't you think?"

She knew she was falling in love with Brent, and she also knew love came along maybe once in a lifetime if you were lucky. Her mother had been twice blessed, but not everyone was. Amira knew what she felt for Brent was special, and if she stayed here and didn't go with him, she'd regret it for the rest of her life.

"I don't know what I'll tell the queen."

He continued to stroke her cheek as if he garnered as much pleasure from it as she did. "I'm sure you'll think of something. You could tell her you're seeing some of the state while you're here. That's true."

Yes, it was. And the queen *had* told her she should see the sights. "I'll have to give her the number at…Shady Glenn, is it?"

"That's no problem. Do you really think she'll be calling?"

"Only if there's something new to report. I can check in with her secretary and then she won't worry about me."

"So you'll go?"

She realized the decision had been made as soon as he'd asked. "Yes, I'll go."

They were gazing at each other, and neither of them seemed to be able to look away until Cocoa barked a few times.

Brent chuckled. "I'll translate for her. She says to pack light and to bring jeans and sweaters."

"I don't have any jeans along. When do you want to leave?"

"Whenever you're ready."

"Can I have a couple of hours to go shopping first?"

"Sure. I can even recommend a few stores."

Amira's phone rang then. Cocoa trotted over to the instrument and barked at it as if she didn't welcome the intrusion, either.

"I have to get that," Amira apologized. "It might be the queen...or my mother."

Brent nodded, but she could tell from the look in his eyes that he really didn't understand her being on-call and what this mission to find Marcus Cordello meant to Penwyck.

After she picked up the receiver, a strong masculine voice asked, "Miss Corbin? This is Cole Everson."

Cole Everson, the head of the Royal Intelligence Institute, had coordinated the efforts to find Marcus Cordello and his brother. "Hello, Mr. Everson. The queen told me you might be phoning. Have you found a picture yet?"

Out of the corner of her eye, Amira noticed Brent take Cocoa into her sitting area and stand by the window.

"Unfortunately, I haven't. This man protects his privacy with a vengeance and so does everyone else around him. I can't even get hold of a home address. Mail that doesn't go to his business is sent to a P.O. box. I've decided to initiate surveillance on the P.O. box so we can follow whoever picks up the mail to wherever Marcus Cordello lives. I understand he's going to be out of the city this week."

"That's what his secretary told me, and I don't think it was a ploy. She seemed sincere."

There were a few moments of silence. "I discussed

this with the queen, Miss Corbin, and if you'd like to return to Penwyck, I can find someone else to try to meet with the man.''

"Is that what the queen wants?''

"I think the queen wants what's best for you. If you'd rather not be in Chicago alone for a week, or feel this is getting too frustrating for you—''

"I want to do this for Queen Marissa and King Morgan,'' she told Cole. Glancing at Brent, she saw he was watching her intently. "I'm going to take the next few days as a…holiday and see some of the countryside. I'll inform the queen's private secretary where I can be reached.''

"When will she have that information?'' he asked.

"Later today.''

"All right. If I need to contact you, I'll get it from her. I'm hoping to have a photograph by the end of the week. Cordello attended a private school and graduated when he was sixteen. I'm trying to obtain a yearbook from the school. If we can just get that, I'll have an artist age his features properly so you can at least know what he looks like now.''

"Mr. Everson, is Marcus Cordello a recluse?''

"No. He just guards his privacy and the details of his life carefully. That's not unusual in men of his wealth and stature. Tabloids can get hold of photos and use them to their own benefit. But we'll track something down. That's my job. By the time you return to the city, I should have a home address for him, too. In the meantime, you have a good holiday. Will you be needing an escort or a guide? I'm sure the queen will provide one.''

"No. I don't need an escort. I'll be staying at

a...guest house someone recommended. I'll be quite safe.''

"You're sure about this, Miss Corbin? A young woman alone in a strange country—"

"I'm sure, Mr. Everson."

"All right, then. As soon as I have more information, I'll be in touch."

After she hung up the phone, Amira crossed to the sitting area where Cocoa was sniffing the rug and the furniture and anything else that looked interesting.

"What was that all about?" Brent asked, looking concerned.

"Just an update from the head of the Royal Intelligence. He's trying to find a home address for Mr. Cordello. They're going to stake out his post office box."

Brent glanced out the window as if he was looking for the man himself. "I see. Did I hear you mention something about a photograph?"

"Mr. Everson is having trouble locating one. He's hoping to have something by the end of the week. When I told him I was going to take a holiday, he wondered if I wanted an escort or a guide."

At that Brent turned from the window and gazed at her. "What did you tell him?"

"That I don't need one."

"And that you're staying at a guest house."

"Yes. I'll be a guest at your house, right? I don't want to mislead the queen, but...she just wouldn't understand. Neither would my mother."

Approaching her slowly, Brent held her gaze with his. "Are you sure you want to come with me? I don't want you to do anything you'll regret."

"This is my decision to make, Brent, no one else's. I'm sure."

Marcus felt guilty as hell. He'd known what that conversation with Everson was all about, and as soon as Amira had hung up, he'd considered telling her the truth. But if he did, that would be the end of whatever was starting between them. He wanted this week with her. He wanted it more than he'd ever wanted anything in his life. If he told her who he was now, she'd call the queen...she'd call Everson. Lord knew who else she'd call. His life, as well as his brother's and his parents', might never be the same. Any sparks between him and Amira would smother in the ashes of the search for twins and royal obligations. He didn't understand royal obligations, and he didn't want to be any part of them.

So instead of telling her his true identity, he offered, "Fritz will drive you to wherever you want to shop and then bring you back here to pack. I'll try to clear my desk so I can leave the city with a free mind."

As free as it could be, knowing that when they returned, they'd both have to deal with Marcus Cordello.


"This is beautiful country," Amira said as Fritz drove her and Brent to Shady Glenn. "The leaves are gorgeous!"

"Oaks and maples, sycamores and elms. Fall is always a spectacle here. I never tire of this drive."

He might never tire of the drive but the drive was tiring him out, she noticed. He was pale again, and lines of fatigue etched his brow. No matter how hardy he said he was, he needed time to recover from the knife wound and the mugging.

Amira thought about Princess Anastasia, her best friend at the palace, and how well she'd recovered from the unexpected trauma in *her* life. Anastasia, who was five years older, had taken Amira under her wing when Amira and her mother moved there. Everyone had been worried about Anastasia the last few weeks. She'd been in a plane crash and had gone missing. Thank goodness Jake Sanderstone had found her. Although amnesia had complicated their relationship, she and her knight in shining armor had found the kind of love that would last a lifetime…the kind of love Amira dreamed of.

The kind of love she was beginning to feel for Brent?

Concerned for him, she hoped his father might convince him to take it easy for a few days.

About an hour away from Shady Glenn, they stopped at a pleasant restaurant for dinner. Amira noticed how Brent always turned the conversation away from himself, and she wished he'd let down his guard a little. She wished he'd let her get to really know him.

They arrived at Shady Glenn as darkness fell over the rolling hills. Fritz parked beside the old three-story stone house, which was surrounded by blue spruce. Floodlights illuminated the outside of the house, and Amira could see its high double-wide windows and the broad front porch with dark brown railing and balustrades. A detached garage sat at the end of the gravel drive.

"It's elegant," she said simply.

Brent attached Cocoa's leash so the dog wouldn't

run off into strange territory. "I've never thought about it that way. It was always just home. Even after we moved to the city, I thought of it as home."

"Maybe that's because you were your happiest here."

That brought his gaze to hers. "I guess. We were a family here, and my brother and Dad and I still are."

"And your mother?"

He stared at the front door of the house as if he was seeing his mother there. "My mother is never satisfied with what she has. She's on her fifth marriage."

Glancing back at Amira, he asked, "You said your mother remarried?"

"Yes. But I like Harrison. I didn't know how much I missed having a father until he married my mother. When they return from their honeymoon, I'm hoping the three of us can spend more time together."

Fritz had taken their luggage from the trunk while they were talking and now went ahead of them to the porch steps. Brent climbed out of the car with Cocoa and came around to the passenger side, opening Amira's door. They walked up the brick path to the house.

A few moments later they were standing inside. Amira didn't think she'd ever seen a house that looked more inviting. The furniture was large and overstuffed in colors as bright as the rainbow. Braided rugs were surrounded by beautiful, polished hard-wood floors. There was a full-size quilt hanging on one wall, and Amira went over to it, studying the workmanship.

"This is beautiful," she murmured.

"My grandmother, my father's mother, made it

along with some of the stitcheries you'll see on the walls upstairs.'' There were a few paintings of pastoral scenes and a copper sculpted flight of birds hanging beside one of them.

''I thought Dad would be here by now. I'm going to check the machine. My cell phone signal is weak in this area.''

Amira wandered around as Brent went into what she presumed was the kitchen.

He was back a few moments later, a scowl on his face. ''I have some news that might change your plans. My father's been delayed for a few days, some type of management crisis. That means you won't have a chaperone here.''

Amira's pulse beat faster. ''What about Fritz?''

''I keep a car in the garage. Fritz is going to take a few days off and visit family in the area. We'll be here alone.''

Was there really a message from Brent's father? Had he planned this? Did she know him well enough to trust him?

''I know what you're thinking, but I *didn't* plan this. Do you want to hear the message?''

Instantly she felt guilty for her thoughts. Why couldn't she trust her instincts with Brent? Maybe because he was still so guarded. ''No. I don't need to hear the message.''

''I can have Fritz drive you back to Chicago if that's what you want.''

She saw how tired Brent looked, remembered how kind he'd been to her the past few days, recalled every detail of every one of his touches and kisses. She almost felt as if it were her duty to take care of him.

Because she cared about him so much?

She felt a lot more than duty. Over the years in the palace, she'd learned about loyalty and faithfulness and always being ready to serve. But all these feelings for Brent took everything she'd learned to a new realm. Still, she shouldn't make a rash decision. She'd been taught that, too.

"I'll stay the night and decide what happens after that in the morning. I can always hire a driver to take me back." They weren't too far from De Kalb and she suspected there was a car service there.

"That sounds good to me." Brent looked relieved.

Fritz interrupted them as he came down the stairway. "Sir, I took the luggage upstairs. The master bedroom is made up, but the other two aren't."

"That's all right, Fritz, I'll take care of it. You get going."

"Thank you, sir. I'll check on the Jaguar before I leave. It was serviced two weeks ago and it should be in great condition. But I'll make sure."

"I'm sure it's fine. Tell Estelle I said hello."

"I will, sir." He gave Brent a smile and then headed for the door.

Brent glanced at the stone fireplace. "Would you like a fire?"

She could imagine sitting in front of the crackling fire with Brent and no one else around except Cocoa. She wasn't sure she should take the chance and put them in temptation's way. Not tonight.

"I think I'm going to turn in early." Maybe if she did, he would, too. He certainly needed the rest.

"All right. I'll go make up your bed then."

"You know how to make beds?" she teased.

"When my brother and I were kids, we had chores

just like everyone else. Do *you* know how to make up a bed?''

She grinned at him. ''I didn't move into the palace with my mother until I was ten. Like you, I knew the realities of running a home. Even at the palace I make up my own bed so Delia doesn't have to.''

''Who's Delia?''

She felt a bit embarrassed by admitting, ''She's sort of a valet for both me and my mother. She keeps our rooms clean, makes sure my clothes are pressed. That sort of thing.''

''It seems you and I have a lot in common,'' he said pensively as he started up the stairs.

Brent showed Amira to a pretty room decorated in shades of aqua and yellow. The curtains were lacy as was the bedskirt. The Aubusson rug on the floor showed wear, but was still very beautiful.

''I'll be right back,'' he said.

In a few minutes he brought sheets and a blanket to the room. Removing the patchwork quilt, he laid it over the cane-back rocker. Together they made the bed. When he stretched the blanket across the top sheet, his gaze caught hers. They went to smooth out a wrinkle at the same time and their fingers brushed. Backing away, Brent lifted the quilt from the rocker.

As he tossed it across the bed, he grimaced.

Amira warned, ''You shouldn't be doing this.''

''I'm not an invalid,'' he brusquely reminded her once more and tossed the pillows on top of the quilt.

''No, you're not. But you were hurt only three days ago, and you're trying to act as if it didn't happen. You can't do that, Brent.''

He faced her with his jaw set. ''Why not?''

''Because you need time to heal. You're not a superhero, even though I forget that sometimes,'' she added with a smile.

His annoyance dissipated, and he slowly came around the bed and took her hands in his. ''You're very good for me, Amira. When I'm with you, I feel peaceful. I haven't felt that way in a very long time.''

''Do you only feel peaceful?'' she asked tentatively, not knowing if she should.

''If only you knew,'' he murmured as he folded his arms around her, bringing her close to him. ''In one sense I feel peaceful. In another…''

He let his words trail off as he lowered his head and covered her lips with his. She knew in every kiss he was acknowledging how innocent she was, how inexperienced. He seemed to use that to awaken the fire in her, to awaken passions she never knew she'd feel. His tongue taunted her upper lip, and she tightened her arms around him. Then he angled his head so he could take the kiss deeper, and she moaned softly, feeling prickles of fire in every part of her, longing for satisfaction she'd never known. The pure sensuality of his hands passing up and down her back, his scent, his slow, enticing ravishment of her mouth weakened her knees and made her feel as if she were drowning in Brent.

Suddenly he stopped all of it and lifted his head. ''I don't know what this week's going to bring, but I do know I won't take advantage of you. I want you to realize what you're doing every step of the way. Since we don't even know if you're going to stay, I think I'd better go to my room.''

She admired so much about Brent Carpenter—his honesty, his sincerity, his kindness. He was real yet noble, as noble as the soldiers who protected the king, as noble as the military who fought to keep Penwyck free.

Should she stay here alone with him or shouldn't she? If she did, she knew what might happen. She welcomed the thought of truly loving Brent, yet she didn't know much about him. What if he often picked up women and brought them home? What if she wasn't special to him? What if she gave her heart and he kept protecting his?

"Have you ever been seriously involved in a relationship?" she asked him.

Stepping away from her, his face changed, and she could no longer see the desire in his eyes. She could see nothing there now and that scared her.

"Yes, I've been seriously involved. But I don't want to discuss it, Amira. It has nothing to do with you and me being here now."

"I don't think that's true," she protested. "Whatever happened in your past shaped who you are, just as mine shaped me. While we're here, I'd like to get to know you better. Isn't that why you asked me along?"

His response was quickly emphatic. "No. I asked you along so we could enjoy each other's company, go out on the lake, appreciate the children."

"And?" she prompted, knowing what else was on his mind because it was on hers.

"And...maybe do whatever comes naturally to a man and a woman."

Suddenly she had to know the truth. "Did you bring me here to seduce me?" she asked bluntly.

At first she saw anger flash in his eyes, but it disappeared and all that was left was exasperation. "Where is this coming from?" he asked. "I told you

I won't take advantage of you. If and when we have sex, we'll both want it. Seduction isn't part of that.''

"I see," she said softly, more confused than ever. He wouldn't seduce her, but he wanted to have sex with her. He wanted her company, but he didn't want to go any deeper than surface chatter.

Cocoa ran up the steps then and into Amira's room.

"I'd better take her out for a walk," Brent said gruffly. "Feel free to turn in. I'll keep her with me."

There had been a wall around Brent before, but it had cracked here and there and she'd seen glimpses into his soul. Now it seemed he'd patched up all the cracks and she couldn't see into him at all. Maybe she should leave in the morning…or maybe she should work at tearing that wall down.

"I'll see you in the morning, then," she murmured.

"In the morning."

When he left her room, he shut the door. She felt he'd also shut it on the feelings that were growing between them because maybe they were just too uncomfortable for him to handle.

# Chapter Six

When Amira came downstairs the following morning, Brent was already sitting at the kitchen table, a mug of coffee in front of him, Cocoa at his feet. "Instant," he said, grimacing. "If we want breakfast, we'll have to buy groceries. I waited in case you'd like to come along."

Cocoa ran to Amira, and she bent down to pet her. "Where do we have to go?"

"About two miles up the road there's a general store. They sell a little bit of everything. You might enjoy the uniqueness of it. Even if you decide to go back to the city, you need to eat before you go."

She latched on to the practicality of that. "I'd like to see your general store."

Standing, he took his cup over to the sink and dumped the coffee down the drain. "Nice outfit," he said with a nod and a hint of a smile.

Because she wasn't used to wearing the type of clothes she'd put on, she felt a bit self-conscious. The royal-blue leggings hugged her body from her waist to her ankles. Her cashmere sweater was the same color blue, short, only coming to her waist. It swung a little when she walked. According to the salesclerk, the black, tie-shoes on her feet were all the rage. They felt a bit clompy to her, but fashion was fashion.

"It feels a little bit odd," she admitted.

"What do you wear when you attend classes?"

"Slacks and sweaters. Nothing like this. It would raise more than a few eyebrows."

"Do you have men in those classes?"

"Sure we do."

"Then it would raise a few temperatures, too."

She knew she was blushing and couldn't help it. "Are we taking Cocoa?" she asked, changing the subject because it reminded her too much of what they'd said to each other last night.

"We'd better leave her here. They might not let her inside. She'll be fine. I'll go get the car. Just turn the button on the knob and the door will lock when you shut it."

After Amira found her sweater in the living room, she said goodbye to Cocoa, then locked the door and waited for Brent. They rode to the general store in silence. She felt a tension between them this morning—a different kind of tension than the one that had hung between them since they'd met. It had to do with her decision to stay or go, with her question last night about Brent's serious relationship. He obviously didn't want to reveal anything about his personal life. If she stayed, maybe she'd figure out why.

The general store was a clapboard building situated next to a gas station. Four concrete steps led to the

# How To Play:

1. With a coin, carefully scratch off the 3 gold areas on your Lucky Carnival Wheel. By doing so you have qualified to receive everything revealed—2 FREE books and a surprise gift—ABSOLUTELY FREE!

2. Send back this card and you'll receive 2 brand-new Silhouette Romance® novels. These books have a cover price of $3.99 each in the U.S. and $4.50 each in Canada, but they are yours ABSOLUTELY FREE.

3. There's no catch! You're under no obligation to buy anything. We charge nothing—ZERO—for your first shipment. And you don't have to make any minimum number of purchases—not even one!

4. The fact is thousands of readers enjoy receiving books by mail from the Silhouette Reader Service™. They enjoy the convenience of home delivery…they like getting the best new novels at discount prices, BEFORE they're available in stores… and they love their *Heart to Heart* subscriber newsletter featuring author news, horoscopes, recipes, book reviews and much more!

5. We hope that after receiving your free books you'll want to remain a subscriber. But the choice is yours—to continue or cancel, any time at all! So why not take us up on our invitation, with no risk of any kind. You'll be glad you did!

**A surprise gift**

# FREE

**We can't tell you what it is…but we're sure you'll like it! A**

# FREE GIFT!

**just for playing LUCKY CARNIVAL WHEEL!**

Visit us online at
www.eHarlequin.com

# LUCKY

Find Out Instantly The Gifts You Get **Absolutely FREE!**

# Carnival Wheel

### Scratch-off Game

Scratch off
**ALL 3**
Gold areas

## YES! I have scratched off the 3 Gold Areas above.
Please send me the 2 FREE books and gift for which I qualify! I understand I am under no obligation to purchase any books, as explained on the back and on the opposite page.

### 315 SDL DNW9                    215 SDL DNW3

| | |
|---|---|
| FIRST NAME | LAST NAME |

ADDRESS

| APT.# | CITY |
|---|---|

| STATE/PROV. | ZIP/POSTAL CODE |
|---|---|

# The Silhouette Reader Service™—Here's how it works:

Accepting your 2 free books and gift places you under no obligation to buy anything. You may keep the books and gift and return the shipping statement marked "cancel." If you do not cancel, about a month later we'll send you 6 additional novels and bill you just $3.34 each in the U.S., or $3.80 each in Canada, plus 25¢ shipping & handling per book and applicable taxes if any.* That's the complete price and — compared to cover prices of $3.99 each in the U.S. and $4.50 each in Canada—it's quite a bargain! You may cancel at any time, but if you choose to continue, every month we'll send you 6 more books, which you may either purchase at the discount price or return to us and cancel your subscription.

*Terms and prices subject to change without notice. Sales tax applicable in N.Y. Canadian residents will be charged applicable provincial taxes and GST.

If offer card is missing write to: Silhouette Reader Service, 3010 Walden Ave., P.O. Box 1867, Buffalo, NY 14240-1867

SILHOUETTE READER SERVICE
3010 WALDEN AVE
PO BOX 1867
BUFFALO NY 14240-9952

## BUSINESS REPLY MAIL

FIRST-CLASS MAIL    PERMIT NO. 717-003    BUFFALO, NY

POSTAGE WILL BE PAID BY ADDRESSEE

NO POSTAGE
NECESSARY
IF MAILED
IN THE
UNITED STATES

wooden screen door. The inside door was open even though the temperature outside was cool.

Brent went in first and took a quick look around. When he saw the salesclerk, he seemed to relax. He picked up the top plastic basket from a stack inside the door. "What would you like for breakfast?" he asked her.

"Can we make pancakes with blueberries?"

"We can if there are blueberries in that case over there." He pointed to the refrigerated section.

She went to the case and peeked inside like a kid in a candy store, not knowing whether to pick up the blueberries in the box or the ones in the bag.

"I don't do much grocery shopping," she admitted as he came over to join her.

"I don't, either. We make a good pair. We're both out of touch with the real world."

Slanting him a glance, she saw he was serious. "Coming to the United States has given me a whole new perspective on a lot of things."

"Like?" he asked.

"How sheltered palace life is, how much of the world I haven't seen, how much freedom I've never really had…how very protected I've been. This trip, succeeding in meeting Marcus Cordello…it's like a rite of passage for me."

A shadow seemed to cross Brent's face.

"What's wrong?" she asked.

"Nothing. I'm hungry, that's all. I'll pick up a few provisions, then we can go stir up those pancakes."

When they returned to Shady Glenn, Marcus grabbed both bags of groceries and wouldn't let Amira help carry them. Their conversation about the real world had troubled him, reminding him of

Rhonda and the life he'd led with her. She had been hip and sassy, lighthearted and fun. It had been convenient for them to be together, convenient for them to care about each other, convenient to think about a future. She'd loved everything his money could buy her, and he'd loved giving her presents and a taste of his world.

What he regretted was not giving her enough of himself. If he had, she would have told him she had diabetes. She wouldn't have hidden the fact that she had to give herself insulin twice a day. If he'd known about her condition, he would have watched her more carefully.

Everything he was feeling about Amira was bringing back all of the old baggage he'd fought to leave behind.

Amira's questions last night had made him defensive, and he'd handled all of it badly. He'd had to ask himself honestly—had he brought her here to seduce her? The answer to that was yes, so he knew he had to back off, treat her like a friend and answer some of her questions. That's the conclusion he'd come to in the middle of the night.

Cocoa greeted them both as if she hadn't seen them for years.

Afterward Brent found a griddle in one of the cupboards and then started coffee brewing. Silently Amira took a large bowl from a cabinet and began to mix the pancake batter.

Once he'd poured the water into the coffeemaker, he leaned against the counter, deciding to take the bull by the horns. "You asked me last night if I'd ever had a serious relationship."

She stopped stirring.

"When I was twenty-one I was engaged. Her name was Rhonda."

Amira lifted her eyes to his. "What happened?"

Crossing his arms over his chest, he began, "I wish I could tell you we had an argument and went our separate ways. That would have been easier than what happened." He thought about his life a few years ago. "I met Rhonda at a party. I went to a lot of them back then. I was a bachelor looking for a good time, earning a master's degree in finance. Rhonda was in an undergraduate program in the same field so we had a lot to talk about. She was one of those women who never ran out of things to say or suggestions for fun things to do. We had a fast life. I worked at my business during the day, earned my master's at night. She was in her senior year, determined to become an investment banker."

"It sounds as if the two of you fitted together well," Amira said quietly.

"I thought we did. But she didn't tell me something very important about herself, and I still can't decide if that was my fault or hers. She had diabetes and she wasn't taking good care of herself. I didn't know that. I thought she was losing weight because she wanted to be model thin. I didn't realize she sometimes skipped her insulin or didn't eat when she should have. And when I found out, it was too late."

"She became ill?"

He pushed away from the counter and jammed his hands into his pockets. "She passed out in class one day and slipped into a coma. I sat by her bed with her parents for two days, praying and hoping. But her kidneys failed and she died."

"Oh, Brent."

"I felt responsible, Amira. Why wasn't I the type of man she could confide in? Why hadn't I seen what was happening to her? Why hadn't I questioned her more thoroughly about the weight loss? Why didn't I see something was wrong with her?"

Amira took a few steps closer to him. "Did you ever consider that maybe she didn't want you to see?"

"Why not?"

Her violet eyes were wide and steady and compassionate. "For the same reason that you wouldn't admit your shoulder hurt. Why did you have to carry both grocery bags in here today? Why couldn't you let me bring one of them in?"

"I didn't want you to think—'

"That you weren't strong? That you were taking too long to heal? That I'd think less of you if I had to help?"

He'd never talked about this with anyone. His dad and Shane knew what had happened, of course, but he'd never discussed it with them. He'd never told them how devastated he'd felt or how guilty. Now Amira was making him take another look at all of it. "Women don't have an image or ego to protect," he protested.

"Don't they? Oh, Brent. She probably wanted to keep up with you in every way. She wanted to look good for you. She wanted to be what you wanted her to be."

"Then it *was* my fault."

Shaking her head emphatically, Amira protested, "No, it wasn't your fault. Even in Penwyck, girls see magazines, read articles about what men supposedly want. They make themselves into a package. It's only when a woman really trusts a man, deep in her soul, that she can leave off the makeup, dress in sweats and not brush her hair.''

If only he could believe that. If only... "We dated for a year. We were going to get married. She should have trusted me.''

"Did you trust her?''

He thought about that. He'd been building his empire, wheeling and dealing. He and Rhonda had talked about finance, but he'd never told her details of his work. He'd never given her specific names of companies he was working with or thinking about buying. Was that because he thought she might use the information to further her own future? To get herself a better job?

On a deeper level, he had never told her what it had been like to be separated from Shane when they were kids. Yet he'd already told Amira how difficult that had been. He could see himself sitting down with Amira, explaining a merger he wanted to accomplish and letting her bat ideas back to him. And now this conversation they were having...

"I guess I didn't trust her any more than she trusted me. I don't know why. I never told her about Mother and Dad's fights. Or the affair Dad had that broke up my parents' marriage.''

"Maybe you both were trying to be what you thought the other person wanted.''

"This is heavy stuff before breakfast,'' he said gruffly, and went over to the window to look out at the backyard where a wooden swing hung from the tall oak. That swing had been there since he was a child.

Following him to the window, Amira stood very

close, her elbow brushing his. "What do you see out there?" she asked, seemingly out of the blue.

"I see—" He stopped before he said Shane's name. "I see my brother and me climbing the tree, shimmying to the top branches. I can hear our mother telling us we were going to break our necks, and see Dad putting up a ladder against the tree just to be on the safe side." He pointed to a patch of land in the rear corner. "See that area that looks like it's over-grown with vines?"

Amira nodded.

"Every June my mom and my brother and I would pick strawberries. When Dad came from the city on weekends, we'd make ice cream on the front porch and put the strawberries over it. I guess it's silly now to think about that, but I do often."

"That's because you were happy then."

Turning away from the window, he left the past and found the present. "I haven't been happy for a long time. I've been busy—not happy."

"And you haven't been involved with anyone since Rhonda?"

"No. After she died, I decided personal relation-ships carried too high a price. Being responsible for another person's life and happiness is just too great a burden." He still believed that even now. That's why he'd wanted Amira to come and spend this week with him. He wanted to be happy without the responsibility of thinking about the future…because there could be no future between the two of them.

After she studied his face, she quietly said, "I know loving can sometimes be a burden. But when I hear my mother talk about my father, I know she would have given up anything for that love. Seeing her with Harrison now, I can tell she's found love all over again and the two of them complete each other's lives.''

Brent shook his head. ''I only see heartache when two people connect. My family broke up because my father turned to another woman and my mother found out. Because they couldn't repair their marriage, they separated me from my brother. Rhonda and I cared for each other, but apparently not deeply enough.''

He paused for a moment, then asked very soberly, ''What does it take to make a successful relationship? What kind of love do you have to have? I don't know, Amira. Most of the time I believe men and women are supposed to be ships passing in the night. It's much easier that way. Last night you asked me if I brought you here to seduce you, and I got angry because you put it into words. I did bring you here for that. But I promise you now, if you stay, we'll become friends before anything else happens. I don't want you to have regrets when you go back to Penwyck.''

Gazing into her eyes, he could see what her answer would be before she said it. ''I'll stay.''

He knew it took courage for her to make that decision. She was going against an upbringing that would make staying alone in a house with a man a scandal. But she wanted more time with him as much as he wanted it with her.

More than anything, he wanted to take her into his arms and kiss her, yet he knew kissing could easily get out of hand and he intended to keep his word to her. ''Let's go for a walk after breakfast. I want to show you everything I like best about being here.''

Before he realized what she was going to do, she

rose up on her tiptoes and kissed his cheek. That simple gesture touched him in a way nothing else could. "What was that for?"

"Your honesty. Our friendship."

His honesty. What would happen when she found out he was Marcus Cordello?

Right now it didn't matter. For the next week he was Brent Carpenter.

And he'd deal with the rest later.

At first Brent captured all of Amira's attention as they went out the back door and through the yard. The blue sky had become overcast and there was dampness in the air. But she hardly noticed all that. Her world was filled by the man beside her who had finally given her a piece of his soul. She could understand better now why he closed himself off and had been slow to share personal information. Several times in his life, he'd had to fit the puzzle pieces back together again.

Now she could understand why he immersed himself in his work and hadn't looked for another serious involvement. He wasn't looking for one now. He felt responsible for his fiancée's death, even though he wasn't. Love brought with it responsibility so he didn't want either. Amira knew she had to take this week for what it was, an interlude—time to spend with a man she was beginning to care about deeply. She had to accept the fact that that was all it was. Could she do that?

As Brent's large hand clasped her elbow, she didn't have time to formulate an answer. "Over this way," he directed her.

Cocoa ran beside them as they came to the end of

the pathway in the yard and entered a copse of weeping birches.

"Through here." Brent's hand went to the small of her back.

She could feel its imprint through her sweater. She felt small beside Brent, protected by him, excited by being so close.

"Where are we going?"

"In a few minutes you'll see," he said with an easy grin.

Emerging from the birches, they came into a small clearing bordered by pines. In that clearing sat a lopsided little building that Amira supposed could be a utility shed. Except, she could make out a shade at the window, and the door was somewhat unusual. It was a Dutch door such as she'd seen at a stable. Then she saw the slab of wood nailed above the door. It looked as if it had seen many winters. She could just make out the letters that spelled Private and she suddenly knew what it was.

"You had a clubhouse."

"A clubhouse for two. My brother and I built it. We found the plans in a magazine and it gave us something to do the summer we were eleven."

"May I?" she asked motioning toward the door.

"You'd better let me open it first and see if it's safe to go inside."

When Brent opened the door, there were only a few cobwebs and the smell of damp leaves. "You're too tall to fit," she teased.

He stooped, then folded his legs and sat on the floor. When he patted the boards next to him, she laughed and ducked through the doorway.

Then she sat on the floor beside him with their

shoulders brushing. Cocoa wiggled inside beside Brent and settled on the wooden floor, too.

"You and your brother did a good job if this is still standing," Amira remarked.

"It's been through a few repairs, but it's held up well."

In the small quarters Brent was more than ever aware of her. He took her hand in his and held it, interlacing their fingers. The silence was only broken now and then by birds chirping and by the breeze blowing stray leaves across the threshold.

"I spent a lot of time here," he said. "Although my brother was far away, I felt closer to him in here."

"Did you live at Shady Glenn all year round?"

"Before the divorce, yes. After the divorce, my father got an apartment in the city and we stayed there during the week and came out here on weekends. After he remarried, I didn't get home for months at a time."

"Why? Where were you?"

"At boarding school…prep school…whatever you want to call it. Someplace where my stepmother didn't have to deal with me."

Her indignation caused her cheeks to flush. "That's a *terrible* thing to do to a child. Didn't your father realize that?"

Brent shrugged. "My dad wanted to keep peace with his new wife. By the time I was ready for college, they'd separated and divorced, too. The truth is, I don't think my dad ever stopped loving my mom. If she'd been able to forgive his affair, they might still be together."

Amira was quiet for a while. "When trust is broken, it's difficult to get it back again."

Brent thought about his first night with Amira and why he hadn't told her he was Marcus Cordello. "There are reasons why people do the things they do. There are always two sides…two points of view."

"I guess if two people love each other enough, they can overcome anything," Amira mused.

Cocoa had put her nose on Brent's leg. Her eyes were closed, and to lessen the intensity of the moment, Amira nodded to her. "I think we tuckered her out."

"Just as well. That means we'll have a few moments of privacy," Brent said, his voice low and intimate. Taking Amira's chin into his hand, he tilted her face up to his.

When he kissed her, she felt there was a new depth to it, a richness that hadn't been there before. Maybe it was because of everything he'd shared with her. Maybe it was because their friendship was growing into so much more…at least on her part.

Suddenly there was the rat-tat-tat of rain on the roof.

Cocoa scrambled to her feet, and Brent lifted his head. "Uh-oh. We'd better make a run for it."

Holding on to the leash with one hand, Brent hurried out of the clubhouse and held his hand out to Amira. "Come on. If we hurry, we might not get soaked."

Brent held Amira's hand as they ran. Moments after the drizzle started it changed to a downpour. When they reached the back door to the house, Brent held it open for Amira and she rushed inside.

Cocoa purposely shook, and water splattered everywhere.

"I'm not much better than Cocoa," Amira said. "I'm dripping all over your floor."

With a smile Brent nodded to the bathroom. "Go ahead and get out of those clothes. I'll light a fire, then change in the laundry room. I have a pair of jeans in there."

Cocoa trotted behind Brent to the living room.

Amira had stripped off her clothes in the downstairs bathroom when she suddenly realized she had nothing to put on. Not only that, but her hair was wet and she needed to brush it out while she dried it or it would frizz all over.

Wrapping herself in one of the bath towels, she opened the door and peeked out. She thought she heard the dryer door close in the laundry room. She could scurry upstairs, put on fresh clothes, then do something with her hair.

But she'd barely made it to the stairway when she heard Brent's footsteps. Before she could start up the steps, he was there, his gaze raking over her as he took in her bare shoulders, the towel tucked at her breasts, her bare legs and feet.

"Come sit by the fire," he said, his voice husky. "I'll go get you some clothes."

She hadn't even noticed the kindling taking off in the fireplace. Her hand went to her hair. "I need to fix up a little."

"You don't need to fix a thing. Go on. Sit on the sofa and cover up with the afghan. Do you want jeans?"

"I laid a sweat suit over the chair upstairs. That'll be fine."

He couldn't seem to take his eyes off her, and she couldn't stop staring at his chest. He was shirtless and so very masculine. His shoulders were so broad. The dark brown hair running down the middle of his chest whirled around his navel. He hadn't even snapped his jeans, she realized, and quickly brought her gaze back up to his. The fire couldn't be warming the room already, but she felt very hot, very excited, very…much a woman.

Breaking the silence, he murmured, "I'll be right back," and then he was up the stairs, and her knees were shaking as she made her way to the sofa where she curled up in the corner and covered herself with the afghan. Only this morning they'd spoken of being friends first…before anything else happened between them. Yet their attraction to each other, the pull toward each other, was stronger than logic or good intentions.

Her heart beat faster as she heard Brent's footsteps in the upstairs hall, heard him descend the steps. Suddenly he was standing before her with her clothes. She noticed his eyes dipped to her breasts covered modestly by the afghan. Then his gaze returned to her face. There was such a deep need and longing there in his eyes.

He held out the clothes to her, and his voice was husky. "I'll go into the kitchen. Let me know when you're dressed."

She could let him walk away. She could build on their friendship. She could get dressed and pretend she didn't feel the longing and the need, too. But was that honest when all she wanted was to be held in his arms? When all she wanted was to let him awaken every womanly desire she'd never felt?

Taking the clothes from him, she set them aside. "Will you kiss me?"

"Amira." His voice was a pleading groan, telling her she was pushing him too far. "You don't know what you're asking. I can't turn my desire for you on and off like a light switch."

"Then don't turn it off," she suggested softly.

Sinking down on the sofa beside her, he took her into his arms, afghan and all, kissing her eyes, her nose, trailing kisses down her cheek to her neck.

"You are so sweet," he murmured. "Like a Christmas gift someone surprised me with when I didn't believe in Christmas any longer. I can't wait to unwrap you." Keeping his eyes on hers, he reached for the corner of the afghan that had been thrown over her shoulder. He'd almost uncovered her breasts when the phone rang.

He swore. "I'll let it ring."

But when it rang a second time, Amira looked worried. "It could be for me. If it is, I should answer it."

The expression on Brent's face changed from desire-filled to remote, and he shifted away from her. "I have Caller ID. I'll check it. If it's not someone I recognize, you can pick it up."

While Brent went to check the phone on a small bench by the dining room, Amira quickly wrapped the afghan around her again.

"It's for you. It's an international area code that I don't recognize."

Making sure the afghan was securely fastened around her like a huge bath sheet that dropped to her ankles, she knew only her shoulders were showing. Yet as she moved toward the phone, she had the afghan wound so tightly that she knew Brent could see every curve and every wiggle. When she picked up the receiver, he moved away, over to the window and stared out at the rain.

"Hello?" she said, not knowing who to expect.

"Hi, darling."

"Mother! It's so good to hear your voice. Are you still in Greece?"

"We've been out on a sailboat Harrison hired for the past three days. Now we're on Santorini. There are cafés, vineyards, black sand beaches. Our suite has a view of the Aegean Sea. It's so beautiful, Amira. I wish you could see it."

"Maybe I will someday," she murmured, thinking how perfect the Greek island sounded for a honeymoon.

"How are you getting along? When I called the palace, Mrs. Ferth gave me this number."

"I'm not in Chicago right now. I haven't seen Marcus Cordello yet. He's on vacation somewhere this week and nobody knows where. So I thought I'd take a holiday until he comes back."

"That's a wonderful idea. Except you're all alone. Are you sure it's safe?"

"Oh, it's safe. I'm in the country at this wonderful house. It's raining now and there's a fire going."

"Won't you be lonely?"

"Oh, no. Really, Mother, it's a treat. Doing what I want, when I want to."

"Sometimes I worry about you, honey. I didn't realize how lonely *I* was until I met Harrison. Now I know the rest of my life, I'll never be alone again. I love him so much. More each day. I can hardly imagine my life before I met him anymore."

Amira could hear the happiness in her mother's voice and it made her heart ache. She glanced over at Brent. What had she been about to do? She knew he didn't want a serious relationship. She knew after she accomplished her mission, she'd never see him again unless she flew to the United States or he flew to Penwyck. They could have a few days together every few months. Once a year? What kind of relationship was that?

"I'm glad you found Harrison, Mother. I'm glad you're not lonely anymore."

"I didn't mean to suggest that being with you, having you, wasn't enough. You understand that, don't you?"

"Of course. The bond between a man and woman isn't like any other."

"You sound as if you know that from experience. Have I been too involved with palace affairs to notice something going on in your life?"

"No. You haven't been too involved. I…I guess I just dream about that kind of bond. You talked about having it with father, and I see you have it with Harrison. It's just something I want, too…along with children." She glanced over at Brent again and saw he was watching her intently.

"You must be careful, Amira. I never told you, but I knew about your meetings with Sean in the garden."

"You never said anything."

"It seemed to end as fast as it started. And you were only seventeen then. Now, at twenty, you might be ready for something more serious. When you're on Penwyck, you have lots of people to look out for you. But on your own in Chicago… Be careful. There are men who would take advantage of a beautiful young woman like you."

Amira was aware she was standing in Brent's living room with only an afghan wrapped around her. A few minutes before she'd welcomed his attentions and encouraged him. Now she felt ashamed that she'd been so bold. Was she mature enough to act on her feelings? Was she mature enough to listen to her heart?

"When will you be flying back to Penwyck?" Amira asked, changing the subject.

"Probably tomorrow. Harrison must get back. We've decided to look for a house in the country but keep Harrison's apartment since it's so convenient to the palace."

"I think when I return, I'd like to find a place of my own."

Silence met her words, then her mother said, "If you think you're ready for that, then that's what you should do. I'd love to go apartment hunting with you."

Amira knew she and her mother would always be close, no matter what happened, no matter how their lives changed. She was so grateful for that. "I'd love for you to help me decorate. Your taste is as good as mine."

Gwen Montague laughed. "You take care of yourself, honey. I hope I see you as well as Marcus Cordello sometime next week."

"I'll do what I can to make that happen. Has King Morgan's condition changed?"

"No. It's the same. All we can do is pray and try to figure out who is the true heir to the throne. Take care, and I'll see you soon."

When Amira hung up the phone, tears pricked her eyes. She missed her mother. She missed everyone at the palace. But most of all she felt as if by being here with Brent, she was becoming a different person. She didn't know what was right and what was wrong, what was best or what would lead her into trouble.

Brent broke into her train of thought. "That was your mother, I take it."

"Yes, she's having a lovely honeymoon, but... she's worried about me." Awkwardly Amira walked to the sofa and picked up her sweat suit. "I'm going to get dressed."

"Amira, we weren't doing anything wrong. You're not a child. You have a right to make your own decisions. Don't let your mother make you feel guilty—"

Amira held up her hand to stop him. "She'd never intentionally make me feel guilty. This isn't about what I should or shouldn't do according to anyone else's standards. It's about me and you and what I want for my life. When I was talking to my mother, I realized I always imagined my first time with a man would be with my fiancé or my husband."

"I can't offer you more than this week," Brent said honestly.

"I know that. That's why I'm going upstairs and getting dressed."

Then she crossed to the stairway with as much dignity as she could muster and let the afghan trail behind her like a train. She could feel Brent's gaze on her as she ascended the steps, and she just hoped she could make it to her room before she started crying.

She wanted more than a week with Brent, but that's all he could give.

At the top of the stairs she paused and glanced over her shoulder. He'd turned away and was staring into the fire. What did he think about her now?

# Chapter Seven

After Marcus made sandwiches and opened deli containers from the general store, he went to Amira's room and knocked. She came to the door without her usual smile, then she rushed in. "I'm sorry, Brent. About what happened earlier. I shouldn't have been so forward. I..."

She was altogether flustered. He could tell she'd showered and dried her hair because it was fluffy and soft around her face. The raspberry-colored sweat suit complemented her creamy complexion.

Unfulfilled desire rushed through him again and he got a grip on it. "I expected your suitcase to be packed."

"It should be," she murmured.

Even though he'd expected it, the thought of her leaving was disagreeable. Frustrated, trying to understand her, he asked shortly, "Can't you put aside what you *should* do for once in your life?"

Her violet eyes were very wide, but she squared

her shoulders. "I have to be true to who I am and what I believe. You said you wouldn't push."

So he had, but he hadn't realized how being close to her, talking with her, staying under the same roof with her would affect him. He felt peaceful one minute and turned inside out the next.

"I made lunch," he said gruffly. "Are you staying for it?"

He saw her lip quiver, and he wished he didn't feel so deeply about everything concerning her. Softening his tone, he added, "The rain stopped. I thought we could take Cocoa to Reunion House after lunch."

"You still want me to go with you?" she asked, as if she expected him to throw her out.

"Of course I want you to go with me. I think you'll enjoy the kids."

She worried her lower lip for a moment. "I'll change and be right down."

"You don't have to change. You look fine the way you are. These are children. They don't care what you're wearing."

Her gaze passed over him as if assessing what he'd said. He was wearing jeans and a black polo shirt. He found that having her look at him with those sparks in her eyes was damn arousing. "Change if you want…or don't. Come down when you're ready." Before she stirred up his insides anymore, he went downstairs.

To Amira the tension between her and Brent as they ate lunch was palpable. He was treating her like a polite stranger, and Amira wished there was something she could do about that. But as she'd told him, she couldn't go against everything she'd been taught or put her dreams aside. She wanted to be more than an object of desire.

When they drove to Reunion House, Cocoa sat on Amira's lap. "I'm going to miss her," Amira said.

"So am I. But the kids will keep her better occupied than we can, and she'll have a backyard where she can run and play. Marilyn loves animals as much as she likes kids. She's always said she wished Reunion House had a mascot. I still wonder about Cocoa's owner, though. Flora's supposed to let me know if anyone calls."

When Brent had spoken of Marilyn, the housemother at Reunion House, Amira hadn't known what to expect. But she instantly liked the lady who came out to meet them on the porch. She was in her forties with short black hair and sparkling hazel eyes.

She gave Brent a hug. "It's been a while." After he agreed that it had been, she leaned back and studied him. "How are you feeling?"

"Almost back to normal," he assured her. "Now I want you to meet somebody. Lady Amira Sierra Corbin, this is Marilyn Johnson, chief mom and bottle washer of Reunion House."

Marilyn gave Amira a comprehensive look that sized her up as she smiled and extended her hand. "It's good to meet you, Lady Amira. Brent told me he'd be bringing you along to show you around."

"Please call me Amira."

Marilyn nodded. "And I'm Marilyn." To Brent, she said, "We have seven children here right now. They'll all love Cocoa." She grinned at the dog that Brent held in his arms and scratched the animal under the chin. "We're so glad to have you here."

Cocoa barked as if she understood exactly what Marilyn had said.

They were all laughing when a pretty young redhead came to the door. "Marilyn, excuse me. I'm sorry to interrupt, but I wanted to know if you want me to put the baked potatoes in the oven for supper tonight."

"It's all right, Joanie. There's somebody here I want you to meet. Our benefactor, Mr...." She stopped. "Brent Carpenter. He's the one who makes Reunion House possible."

Joanie seemed to hesitate only a second before she came outside and stood close to Brent. "How do you do? It's so good to meet you. I just started working here two weeks ago. I know I'm going to love it."

Marilyn explained to Brent, "Joanie has a degree in elementary education, but hasn't been able to find a teaching position yet. She thought Reunion House would be a nice substitute."

Brent put Cocoa down on the porch and shook the young woman's hand. "It's good to have you with us." Then he introduced Amira.

When Joanie took a closer step to Brent, Amira thought it was a proprietary step. She might not be experienced in the ways of men, but she knew the ways of women from growing up with three princesses. Joanie already had a look in her eye that said she was going to get to know Brent better if she had anything to say about it. Amira found herself not liking that idea at all.

Cocoa looked up at Joanie beseechingly as if she wanted the young woman's attention. Joanie scratched the dog's head. "Come on inside." Her smile was mainly for Brent. "I'll introduce you to the kids. There's a great batch of them here right now, except for one little boy who's kind of belligerent.''

''I think we should let Mr. Carpenter make up his own mind about the children,'' Marilyn said wisely.

Joanie blushed. ''Well, sure. They're all in the kitchen having a snack. It's a good time to meet them.''

The rambling old house was spacious and welcoming, and Amira thought anyone could feel at home here. As they crossed the living room, they heard laughter and guffaws coming from the kitchen. There was a shout and what sounded like a dish falling to the floor.

''It sounds like more is going on than snack time,'' Marilyn said with a frown.

They all hurried to the kitchen, Cocoa trailing behind.

Amira knew she shouldn't, but she smiled at the sight of the three girls and four boys participating in a food fight. One of the youngsters dressed in a red oversize T-shirt and baggy jeans—a baseball cap turned backward on his head—stood on one of the chairs, breaking pieces off a cookie. He'd flung a tidbit at one of the girls who squealed and retaliated by tossing a raisin at him. It was the kind of scene Amira would never find in the palace. These kids had energy to burn, and they were doing that instead of repressing it.

Of course the chaos couldn't be allowed to continue.

Marilyn stepped right into it, giving them all a silent reproving look. Shrieks of laughter and food tossing stopped immediately.

Brent nudged Amira's arm and whispered, "Wish I knew how she did that."

Amira could see the amusement dancing in his eyes and she saw the little boy he must have once been before all the changes in his life.

Apparently thinking she should do something with her new position as assistant, Joanie looked up at the boy and said, "Jared, get down from that chair now."

He gave the redhead a defiant look. "We was just having a little fun."

Marilyn shook her head. "What you were doing was making a mess."

He didn't move from the chair, but cast a glance at Brent and then Amira.

Marilyn went over to him. "Jared, if you'd like to get down from there, I'll introduce you to our guests…before all of you clean up the kitchen."

There were groans and grumbles. Jared just gave Marilyn a sheepish look and hopped down to the floor. Then he looked up at her. "Do we really have to clean the kitchen?"

There were crumbs and raisins and bits of cookies from one end to the other. Cocoa was happily licking at them. Unable to see the dog from where he'd been perched, Jared now spotted Cocoa.

Without waiting to hear if he'd have to do unexpected chores or not, he ran over to the dog but didn't get too close. Looking up, he asked Brent, "Is she yours?"

"Not exactly. My friend and I," he nodded to Amira, "found her. Her owner still might claim her. In the meantime I thought she could make some friends here. Would all of you like to take care of her?"

There was a variety of agreeable confirmation that they would.

Picking up Cocoa, Brent directed, "Why don't each of you tell her your name."

Amira decided Brent had chosen a clever way to meet the children, and she listened carefully, too, as Paul, Shara, Jimmy, Glenda, Amy, Mark, and Jared told Cocoa who they were. Brent let each of them pet the dog, and they all did so freely except for Jared. When it was his turn, he hesitated.

Amira stepped closer to the young boy. "She's quite gentle. She won't hurt you if you're nice to her."

Jared's big brown eyes were wary, and he studied Amira for a long time to see if she was telling the truth.

"You saw the others pet her," she reminded him.

"They're them. I'm me. Maybe she won't like my smell."

"There's only one way to find out," Brent said casually.

Beside the plate of cookies on the table was a dish of cheese cubes. Amira picked one up and broke off small pieces. She said to Jared, "Open up your hand."

When he did, she laid the cheese in it. "Just hold it out to her and let her lick it off. She likes table food, but you can't give her too much of it because it might make her sick."

"Dogs get sick?"

"Yes, they do."

Instantly Jared held his hand out to the dog. Cocoa gladly licked up the cheese scraps and Jared's hand, too.

The boy broke into a wide smile. "She likes me."

Paul shrugged. "She likes the cheese."

Everybody laughed, but Jared was petting Cocoa by then, and she was obviously enjoying it.

Joanie went to the closet and took out a broom, dustpan and brush. She handed them to Paul, Glenda and Jimmy. To Jared she said, "You can wet paper towels and wipe off the table. Mark and Shara, you can wash up the dishes."

"Real sport," Jared mumbled under his breath. Amira realized he'd taken a dislike to the younger counselor.

As soon as Joanie had dispensed the chores, she came to stand by Brent's side again. "We'll make sure Cocoa's well taken care of. Would you like to see the bedrooms Marilyn and I wallpapered? We think they're quite an improvement."

"I'd like to give Amira a tour and then I want her to look at the yard outside. She's earning her degree in landscape design and I thought she could give us a few pointers."

"That's an excellent idea," Marilyn agreed. "We could use some color out there and decide where to put a birdbath."

"I ordered a jungle gym. It should be arriving in the next day or so. We'll have to decide the best place for that, too."

"Will it have monkey bars?" Jared asked as he swiped across the tabletop with a paper towel.

"It will have monkey bars and ladders and a rope to climb, too."

As Joanie took Brent and Amira on a tour of Reunion House, she stayed very close to Brent. Amira began to get annoyed. Brent listened to the cute redhead as she explained how she and Marilyn had chosen the wallpaper. She told him they were going to paint the beds and bookshelves, too, in bright colors. But Brent was less interested in the furniture and more interested in the kids.

"I understand Paul and Shara are brother and sister, Glenda and Amy are sisters, Jimmy and Mark are brothers. Who's Jared meeting here?"

"His sister is supposed to arrive tonight." Joanie shook her head. "It'll be a good thing, too. He's a troublemaker."

"Exactly what has he done?" Brent asked.

"He just stirs up the other kids. You saw what he was doing when we went into the kitchen."

"They were all participating in that," Amira interjected.

Joanie gave her a sharp look. "You can bet Jared started it."

"He's probably excited about seeing his sister and has a lot of extra energy," Amira said helpfully, thinking a positive attitude toward Jared would be better than Joanie's negative one.

"Are you around kids much?" Joanie asked.

Amira had to admit she wasn't. "No."

"I have been—between observation field trips and student teaching. Jared's the type of boy who enjoys making trouble."

Thoroughly annoyed with Joanie now, Amira took a deep breath. "Maybe so. But I'd imagine each child has to be treated as an individual. If Jared is acting up, there's probably a reason."

"Well he's not telling any of us what it is. He's quite sullen at times."

The boy hadn't seemed at all sullen to Amira, and she wondered if he was just that way with Joanie.

Joanie placed her hand on Brent's arm. "Let me show you the play stations I've set up. I think you'll approve." Her brown eyes flashed the message that she was quite impressed with him.

Brent looked down at Joanie with a smile. "I'm sure I will."

Amira couldn't tell if he was just being polite or if he was attracted to the teacher. Then she thought about what had happened on the sofa this morning and Brent's needs as a man. With an attractive, willing woman not very far away, how long could he resist?

Amira hated the thought of it, hated the thought of him making love to anyone but her. She realized she was capable of deep, deep jealousy for one very complicated reason. She was in love with Brent Carpenter. She wanted to make love with him more than she'd ever wanted anything, but knowing he didn't want a serious relationship, knowing he didn't want responsibility for anyone other than himself, she knew she'd have to keep her feelings to herself.

During the rest of the tour, Joanie talked animatedly to Brent. Even though he cast Amira a glance every once in a while, she definitely felt like the third wheel.

When they returned downstairs, Joanie took Brent into the living room where there were games and books and CDs. She was showing him the most recent when Amira wandered into the kitchen. The children had finished cleaning up and were outside with Marilyn…except for Jared.

He was standing at the door looking out at all of

them. Not knowing what else to say, she said something obvious. "I'm glad the sun came out again."

He glanced at her and turned to look outside once more. "I can't think of nothin' except seeing my sister."

"How long has it been since you've seen her?"

He shrugged. "A year. My pop ran off and left us. Someone called the cops and they took us away. It's the last I saw her." Facing Amira then, Jared's face broke into a smile. "She's coming tonight."

Amira could see and feel exactly how much this meant to Jared. She could imagine how much it had meant to Brent to be reunited with his brother every summer. He was doing a wonderful thing here with these kids.

"I'm sure your sister can't wait to see you, either. What's her name?"

"Lena. You got any brothers or sisters?" he asked suddenly.

"No, I don't. I often wish I did. I have good friends, though, and that helps."

"It's not the same," he offered with a shake of his head, as if he were much older than ten.

"No, I guess it's not. I'll have to make do, won't I?" She found this little boy engaging, much more mature than his language and his age would predict.

"I wish you were staying here with us instead of Joanie," he mumbled.

"I think I'd like that," Amira responded sincerely. "But unfortunately I'm only visiting for a little while. I don't live around here."

"Where do you live?"

"On an island named Penwyck. It's near Wales. Have you ever heard of it?"

He screwed up his face. "In school. It's over there near England, isn't it?"

"That's exactly where it is."

"That's far away. Maybe someday I'll get to go someplace like that. I want to go to Australia where they have crocodiles."

"It's good to have dreams. If you hold on to them long enough, they'll come true."

"You have to do more than hold on to them," a strong masculine voice maintained.

Amira had been so concentrated on Jared that she hadn't heard Brent come into the room. Now she saw that both he and Joanie were standing at the table.

"You have to do everything you can to *make* them come true," Brent added.

"Like saving up money?" Jared asked.

"That's one way. Learning everything about the place where you want to go is another. Maybe you can learn something in school that could help you get there."

"Like what?"

"Australia has sheep and horses and mines. If you would learn skills that would help with any of those things, someone might hire you over there."

"Really?"

"I'll see if I can find some books on Australia," Brent said. "I'll send them to you. In fact, if I can order them on the Internet when I get back, they might be here by the end of the week."

"Then Lena can read them, too."

Joanie checked the clock above the sink. "It's time for the kids' group session," she said almost apologetically to Brent. "You're welcome to stay if you like."

"I just came over today to give Amira a tour, but I'll be back. The back porch railings need a coat of paint. I have to clean out the spouts, too. I'll be around all week."

And Amira suspected Joanie would be right by his side as often as she could be.

"You going to be here, too?" Jared asked Amira. "I mean longer than today. You can meet Lena."

She made a decision without analyzing it any more. "Yes, I'll be here for a few days, too. I'd love to meet your sister." She glanced at Joanie. "I'll take a more analytical look at the yard the next time we're here."

Brent's gaze settled on her and it was filled with curiosity. But he didn't ask any questions about why she'd decided to stay.

A half hour later when they returned to Shady Glenn, he said, "I can run up to the general store and get steaks for supper. I'll make them on the grill."

She remembered their first night together and sharing a steak. "That sounds good. Maybe I can make something for dessert if you buy a basket of fresh apples."

"You can really cook?"

"Of course I can cook. All I have to do is follow the recipe. I'm not a hothouse flower, Brent. I might have advantages others don't, but no one waits on me hand and foot." It ruffled her feathers to have him think she wasn't just like everyone else, like all the other women he dated or had attracted him before. When he looked at her as an oddity she didn't like it at all.

"Did I strike a nerve?" he asked, brows arched.

"Sometimes I feel as if you're looking at me as if

I'm some kind of specimen. I don't live on another planet."

He fought back a smile. "No, you just live in a palace."

She was beginning to wish she didn't. She was beginning to wish she lived in Chicago.

"It's a building," she said feebly.

Brent rolled his eyes. "A building with a throne room," he teased.

For some reason she was sensitive to all of it right now, and she felt silly tears prick at the back of her eyes. Not wanting him to see, she started for the living room. "Yes, it has a throne room...and a throne...and a king and a queen. Are you satisfied?"

She didn't know where she was going, but her bedroom seemed like a good idea.

Brent caught her before she made it to the stairs. Holding her by the shoulder, he nudged her around. "What's wrong?"

She bit her lower lip, then decided to tell him how she felt about his attitude. "I never minded being part of a royal family until I came here. You're acting as if it's something to ridicule, something that doesn't mean anything at all. It means a lot to me and to our country."

Gently he brushed her hair away from her cheek and looked deep into her eyes. "I'm not ridiculing you. Your life is very different from ours. You've got to admit that. I'm sorry if I poked fun at it. I never meant to upset you."

Amira realized she was more upset about the way Joanie had looked at Brent. "I'm sorry I overreacted."

His gaze was penetrating and questioning as if he

could see something deeper was bothering her. "What made you decide to stay here with me? Spending time with the kids…meeting Jared's sister?"

She could tell him those were the reasons, but those wouldn't be honest. "I'd like to do both. The reason I'm staying though, is because I care about being with you." She remembered what Brent had told Jared about his dreams—that holding on to them wasn't enough. He had to do something about them. She was doing something about her dreams by staying with him.

Brent must have seen her dreams evident in her eyes because he suddenly became very serious. "Amira, I like having you here with me. You know that. And I want you. You know that, too. But don't get starry-eyed about me. It's not practical. We *do* live in different worlds with an ocean between us, and that's not going to change."

She wanted to tell him it could change. She wanted to tell him that she might consider moving her whole world for him. But she knew he didn't want to hear it. She knew if she even broached the subject of love, he'd back off and send her packing.

"I think we can change whatever we want to change if it's important enough."

The phone rang, interrupting their conversation. After a dark glance at it, he went over and checked the Caller ID. "Not anyone I know, so it must be for you. I'll go to the general store and give you some privacy. I won't forget the apples," he added, as he picked up the receiver and handed it to her.

By the time she greeted the caller, Brent had closed the kitchen door.

"It's Cole Everson," the man on the phone stated.

She took a trembling breath. "Hello, Mr. Everson. You have more information for me?"

"Some. I wanted to make contact with you to make sure I had the proper number. We discovered that Cordello's brother's name is Shane, and he's living in California. I decided to go about this one brother at a time. It has to be handled delicately or the whole world will know how upside down everything is in Penwyck. We want to prevent that from happening. Once you make contact with Cordello, I'd like you to convince him to ease our path to his brother."

"I'm sorry I didn't manage to see Marcus Cordello before he jetted away somewhere."

"That's not your fault. From what I understand, this man is as elusive as they come. As I mentioned before, unlike most wealthy men, he stays out of the limelight, no pictures in the newspapers or anything like that."

"Have you found out his home address?"

"Not yet. Apparently no one's fetched his mail from his post office box. If they have, they've been damn good staying out of sight. I should have that picture soon and a few more details. I can overnight everything to you."

When Brent had given her a tour of the house, she'd noticed a fax machine in his office. "There's a fax here. Would that help?"

"That would help a great deal. The photo won't be as good, but you'll get the idea. You have the number?"

"Hold on a minute."

Going into Brent's study, she found the number on the handset of the fax and told Cole what it was.

"We're all set then," he said. "I'll fax it as soon as I have it."

When Amira hung up the phone, she thought about what the next prince of Penwyck might look like. Would he be tall and handsome, befitting the prince's stature?

In a day or two she'd know.

Then again, in a day or two her feelings for Brent Carpenter might overtake her heart completely and she might not even care about the prince of Penwyck.

She'd only care about loving Brent.

# Chapter Eight

Bang! Rustle, rustle.

The loud noise awakened Amira with a jolt. She began to tremble.

Rustle, rustle. Bang.

Someone was climbing the wall. He was coming to kill her and her mother.

Automatically, from fear, panic and practice drills in the palace, Amira dropped to the floor as she'd been taught, seeking cover...seeking refuge. Disoriented, she tried to peer through the blackness all around her. She couldn't see a thing. How close was the assassin? This time her father was gone. He couldn't protect the king or her, her mother...

Still lost in fear, Amira cowered when she heard the rapping on the door.

"Amira? Are you awake?"

She knew that voice. It wasn't the voice of a stranger or anyone in the Royal Guard. It was—

It was Brent. Her heart was pounding so fast she couldn't speak.

The doorknob turned and the banging started again.

Light from the hall streamed into the room through the open door. Brent saw Amira crouched on the floor between the nightstand and the bed. Immediately he hurried to her, hunkering down. "Amira, what's wrong?"

Relief flooded through her, and tears burned in her eyes as she realized she was safe. She wasn't in the palace. She wasn't even on the island. "I...I...nothing's wrong," she finally managed in a whisper.

Reaching out, he clasped her shoulder. "Like hell, it's not. You're trembling."

"It'll pass. It always does."

Apparently, he wasn't going to wait for it to pass, because he helped her to her feet and led her to the bed. After she was seated, he sat beside her, his arm tight around her.

She took a few steadying breaths. "Really. I'm all right."

"You're still trembling," he murmured as he pressed his lips to her temple.

During the years when she was a child and she'd had a nightmare, her mother had held her. They'd come often after her father's death. Since her teen years, she'd handled the panic and the fear herself. She didn't let anyone see her fear of having an assassin kill her the way he had killed her father.

"Why were you on the floor?" Brent asked gently.

"That's what I was taught to do."

"Taught?" he looked totally perplexed.

"There have been assassination attempts on the king."

"At the palace?"

"Yes. At night, if I hear anything strange or running in the halls, shouting or alarms going off, I'm supposed to take cover...find someplace to hide until someone can take me to safety."

"Are you telling me security at the palace has actually been breached?"

"Yes." She cleared her throat, fighting off the remnants of her fears.

"What happened, Amira? Why are you so scared?"

That night was what she didn't want to remember, but apparently blocking it during her waking hours pushed it into her dreams.

"My father was major of the Royal Guard and part of the king's personal contingent. He died intercepting an intruder climbing the wall beneath the king's bedroom window."

"How old were you?"

"Ten. But I wasn't living in the palace then. I remember a soldier coming in the middle of the night. I heard him tell my mother what happened. She went white...she..."

Tears welled up in Amira's eyes and she tried to blink them away. But there were too many of them.

"What happened to the man who killed your father?"

"For years we thought he'd gotten away. After my father was shot, the queen offered my mother the position of lady-in-waiting, and we moved to the palace. The nightmares began then. When the queen learned about my fear, she moved us as far away from the king's chamber as possible. My mother used to hold me at night, and I think she was as afraid as I was that the assassin would climb the wall again and somehow get into our rooms, murdering us like he'd murdered my father.''

"You said for years you thought he'd gotten away. Were you wrong?''

She studied Brent for a long moment and then knew she could confide in him. "I still don't know the whole story, though I think my mother and her new husband do. While I was away on holiday in the Scottish Highlands in August, Owen, one of the royal twins was kidnapped. My mother and Harrison Montague, Admiral of the Navy, got very close and fell in love. He told her the man who killed my father had been wounded the night of the assassination attempt and later died.''

"Why didn't anyone tell you that before?''

"I don't know. It has to do with state secrets and conspiracies. When I learned the man who murdered my father had died, I thought my nightmares would be gone for good. But even after Owen was returned unharmed, I still had them.''

"That's because you're living at the palace. You're still involved in all of it.''

"With Mother married now, I'm going to find a place of my own. I just hadn't found anything suitable before I left.''

"The sooner you move out, the better.''

She shook her head. "The palace has been my home. The royal family has been my family. When the king bestowed the title of lady-in-waiting on my mother for her position with the queen, he bestowed the title of lady on me, too. I was companion to the princesses. Of course, the titles were also given to us because my father gave his life for King Morgan. It's not easy to leave them all.''

Brent's gaze was filled with compassion for her. He brought her into his body, holding her, rocking her. ''Here I thought you were a privileged lady with not a care in the world.'' The wind blew outside, and the banging began again. Amira started and Brent stroked her hair. ''It's just the shutter,'' he said. ''It came loose in the storm. The only way I can get to it is through the window in this room.''

''It's storming?''

Earlier tonight, after dinner, Brent had gone to his study to work, and Amira had come up to her room to read and to write in her diary about all the feelings she was having for him. She'd gone to bed early around ten o'clock.

''It started raining about eleven. But the wind just picked up not so long ago.''

Amira's cheek lay against Brent's bare chest. She loved the feel and the scent of his skin, the taut strength of his muscles, the deepness of his voice. She loved everything about him.

His breath was warm against her temple as he murmured, ''I don't want to ever see you afraid.''

''I'm not afraid while you're holding me,'' she confessed.

''Then maybe I should hold you all night.''

Amira realized she would like nothing better. Brent's hold on her became less comforting and much more sensual. His lips nudged her hair aside as he kissed from her temple down to her ear. She moaned softly at the scalding-hot flickers of his tongue.

''Brent.'' It was a plea. All the fear was gone and

all she could think about was Brent's smell and his taste and his heat.

With erotic care, he tickled her earlobe with his tongue and then sucked it into his mouth. The sensation started a keening ache inside of her. She ran her hand over his chest, sifting through his chest hair, feeling the muscles underneath. When he groaned, she felt power she'd never felt before.

He laid her back on the bed, kissing her face, her eyes, her nose, her lower lip. She laced her fingers in his hair to bring his mouth to hers—

The phone rang.

She went still, and Brent lifted his head. "That better not be the wrong number," he grumbled. Then he pushed himself away from her. After he stroked her hair away from her brow, he said, "I'll be right back."

Amira could hear Brent on the phone, but not what he was saying. She rebelted her robe and went to sit in the cane rocker.

He returned in a few minutes. "It was Marilyn. She's having trouble with Jared."

"What kind of trouble?"

"Jared's sister didn't arrive as planned. Her foster mother had car trouble and they won't get here until tomorrow evening. Jared's afraid she won't come at all, and he won't settle down for the night. Marilyn thinks I might be able to talk him into a calmer mood. I'm going to head over there now."

She thought about the nightmare, about what had just happened with Brent, Jared's eyes as he'd asked her— "Can I come with you?"

"Are you afraid to stay here by yourself?"

Standing, she squared her shoulders. "No. I've

been dealing with these nightmares since I was ten. It's over now and I'm fine. Thank you for comforting me.'' She knew she sounded formal, but she didn't know what else to say.

''Comfort was the least of it,'' he admitted wryly.

''You don't give yourself enough credit. I needed to be held. No one has held me for a very long time. But now it's over, and if I can help with Jared in any way, I'd like to.''

Taking Amira's hand, Brent tugged her into his arms and hugged her. His kiss was light, but the look in his eyes wasn't, and she knew if the phone hadn't rung, they'd be making love right now. Instead, they were going to reassure a little boy that he wasn't alone.

''Is he upstairs?'' Brent asked Joanie without preamble when he and Amira stepped inside Reunion House.

She frowned. ''Yes, and he has everyone else awake, too. I don't know what Marilyn thinks *you* can do when neither of us can get him to settle down.''

''Let's go see.''

Ever since she'd met Jared, Amira didn't like Joanie's attitude toward the boy. It was as if she'd written him off as a troublemaker and didn't even intend to try to help make things better. Amira had noticed she was quite competent and related to the other children well. Maybe it was just a personality clash.

''They're in the playroom upstairs,'' Joanie explained and then glanced at Amira as if she didn't belong there.

Brent was already intent on his mission and started up the stairs.

When Amira reached the second floor, she saw the children gathered in the playroom with Marilyn. The housemother was reading them a story. When Amira listened, she realized it was a passage from *Treasure Island*.

Jared was sitting in a chair, his knees pulled up on the seat, his arms circling them. He was hunched up as if he'd withdrawn into himself, not caring about what was going on around him.

Crossing to Jared, Brent capped the boy's shoulder with his hand.

Marilyn closed the book. "Why don't we all get ready for bed, again."

Jared still didn't look up as Marilyn ushered the boys into their bedroom and Joanie ushered the girls into theirs.

"I think we should talk," Brent told Jared.

"There's nothin' to talk about," the boy mumbled.

"I think there is. You're upset about Lena not arriving and you're taking that out on everybody else. Do you think that's a good way to handle it?"

"What am I supposed to do?" Jared asked defiantly.

"You can start by telling me what's going through your head," Brent suggested.

Jared's gaze met Amira's, and she got the feeling he didn't want her to leave. Sinking down on the floor beside Jared's chair, she crossed her legs. "Sometimes talking helps," Amira offered softly.

"Talking's not going to help. It won't bring Lena here."

"She'll be here tomorrow, Jared," Brent assured him.

"No, she won't! They're just telling me that. I know she's not coming."

"Her foster mother had car trouble. That's all. They'll be here tomorrow around dinnertime."

Jared's eyes met Amira's. "When our pop left, they told us they'd keep us together. They didn't. Why should I believe you?"

"Mr. Carpenter wouldn't lie to you," Amira responded with a certainty she felt.

Jared thought about that for a little while. Then he asked, "I'm supposed to believe she's coming and hold on to it like one of those dreams you told me about?"

She nodded. "Just like that."

After a few moments of silence, he asked, "You really think she'll come?"

"I think she will," Amira assured him.

"Tomorrow night's far away," he mumbled, sounding younger than ten.

Brent crouched down beside him. "I suppose it would help if you had something to make the time go faster. How about a ride on the pontoon boat. Have you ever been fishing?"

Jared shook his head.

"Would you like to go?"

The boy thought about it, then glanced at Amira. "Are you coming, too?"

"Would you like me to come?"

"Yeah." Jared's face reddened a little.

"Then I'll come. I'll pack us a picnic lunch and we can eat on the boat."

"Cool!" Jared said with a grin.

"If you want to go out on the boat with us tomorrow morning, then you're going to have to get some sleep," Brent said firmly.

"Maybe if you have trouble falling asleep, you can count all the fish you're going to catch," Amira suggested.

Jared smiled at them both. "I'll try it. Before, I just couldn't stop thinking about Lena…where she was… not seeing her again…"

Brent straightened. "I know how hard it is to be patient, but you can do it."

When Amira rose to her feet, she saw Joanie standing in the doorway and wondered if she'd heard the whole conversation.

After Jared had bid them good-night and went into the boys' bedroom, Joanie looked up at Brent, her eyes wide, her long lashes giving a little flutter. "You were so good with him. I know if you hadn't come over, we wouldn't have gotten *any* sleep."

There was an element of truth in Joanie's words, but Amira could see through the blatant flattery, too.

Brent just smiled at the young teacher. It was the kind of smile that always made Amira's heart flip, and she was envious of him bestowing it on Joanie now. "Sometimes a little understanding goes a long way. Amira helped. I'm not sure he would have gone out on the boat with me if she hadn't agreed to come along."

"Oh, I'm sure you could have convinced him," Joanie said. "I'll bet you can be very persuasive."

There was an undercurrent in her words that had more to do with the vibrations between a man and woman than convincing a little boy to go fishing.

Brent looked over at Amira. "We'd better be getting back if we're going to get up early. I still have to fix that shutter outside your bedroom.''

Amira thought she saw Joanie's face light up because she'd just learned Amira and Brent weren't sharing a bedroom—they each had their own. Did the young woman think that made Brent fair game?

After Brent talked briefly with Marilyn, he drove Amira back to Shady Glenn. They were silent, lost in their separate thoughts. Brent let Amira out at the door and drove the car to the garage. She went straight up to her bedroom, knowing he'd meet her there to fix the shutter.

Ten minutes later she worried about him as he leaned outside the window, a flashlight and screwdriver in hand.

"Be careful," she murmured, wanting to hold on to him, to make sure he didn't lean too far.

A short while later he pulled his head inside and shut the window. "You worry too much, Amira. I wasn't in any danger of falling out."

"You never know," she murmured.

He came closer to her then, and they both thought about everything that had happened earlier. "Are you sure you'll be able to get to sleep?"

"I'm sure. I'll probably have less trouble than Jared."

Brent gave her one of those smiles like he'd given Joanie. "I think he has a crush on you."

"Don't be ridiculous."

"I'm not being ridiculous. You're a beautiful, kind lady. He couldn't help but fall for that."

Before she could stop herself, she said, "Joanie has a thing for you." She didn't exactly want to call it a crush, because if Brent felt attracted to the woman in any way, it was more than that.

"A thing?" His grin made Amira angry.

"You know what I mean."

"No, I don't."

"Men," Amira said with some disgust, turning away.

But he wouldn't let her escape, and he caught her arm. "Yes, I'm one of them. What makes you think Joanie has a 'thing' for me?"

"I can read women. It's in the way she looks at you, the way she flutters her lashes, the way she stands within six inches of you."

His smile grew wider. "And that bothers you?"

"No." She'd said too much already. Pulling away from him, she went over to her dresser.

Following her, he clasped her shoulder this time, and turned her toward him. "I don't want Joanie, Amira. I want you. More than anything I want to kiss you right now. But if I do that, we'll wind up in that bed and I'm still not sure that's what *you* want."

Earlier she'd been vulnerable. Earlier his comfort had slid into something else. It would have swept her away if the phone hadn't rung. He seemed to know that and she appreciated that about him. Her admiration for him grew every day.

"You're an honorable man, Brent Carpenter."

A shadow passed over his face, and his eyes became sad. "Not as honorable as you think. I wish—" He stopped abruptly.

"What do you wish?"

"I wish lots of things were different." Stepping away from her, he crossed the room to the door. "But they aren't. If you have another bad dream, feel free to call me.''

"I'll be fine." She knew she wouldn't call for him…couldn't call for him. If she invited him into her room again, it wouldn't be for comfort after a bad dream. She'd only invite him into her room again if she decided to make love with him.

"Good night, Amira," he said gently.

"Good night."

When she heard the door to his room close, she sank down onto the bed, knowing any further dreams she had tonight would be of him.

There was a cloud cover when Amira and Brent went to fetch Jared from Reunion House the next morning. It seemed to Amira that a cloud also hung over her and Brent, and she didn't know how to dispel it. Every time he looked at her there was something in his eyes. Sadness maybe? But as soon as she glimpsed it, it was gone and his guard was firmly back in place.

Jared was full of excitement and energy as they walked through the backyard. A Jet Ski bobbed there from the gentle lapping water on the lake. Farther along a blue pontoon boat was moored. It had a circular front deck and high-backed, padded admiral's chairs.

Brent stepped onto the boat first carrying the picnic basket. Jared hopped on before Brent could give him a hand. When it was Amira's turn to board, Brent turned to her and offered her his hand. She took it, feeling such a sense of rightness that it almost overwhelmed her. Whenever she was with Brent, she felt safe. That was so odd since she hadn't felt safe since the night her father had died. Her life in the palace had been pleasant, full of advantages most people didn't have. Yet remembering what had happened to her father, she had never felt safe there. When she'd traveled to Chicago alone, some of that fear had come with her. But when Brent had scooped her into his arms that first night and she lay against his chest, the sense of security had been overwhelming. She realized now that was one of the reasons she was so drawn to him. One of the reasons she'd fallen in love with him.

As Brent helped her into the boat, his arm went around her waist, and he looked as if he was going to kiss her.

"This is so cool," Jared called from under the canopy where he was examining everything. His enthusiasm broke the moment, and Amira stepped away from Brent breathless, knowing this day wasn't about the two of them. It was about keeping Jared occupied.

The breeze ruffled Amira's hair as she sat on one of the chairs, watching Brent teach Jared how to prepare a fishing rod. When Brent's cell phone rang, he grinned at Amira and asked, "Hold this?"

She took the fishing rod, glad that Brent was using corn as bait and not worms. Absently she listened while she watched Jared attach two kernels of corn to his hook.

"The papers have to be signed today?" Brent asked. "All right. I'll be back at the house by five at the latest." He glanced over at Amira. "You've brought Quentin up to speed as far as I'm concerned?" He listened to his secretary for a few moments, then added, "Just tell him not to forget."

A few moments later he attached the phone to his

belt again. Meeting her gaze he explained, "One of my employees is driving up to give me papers to sign."

"Even when you're on vacation you're not really on vacation, are you?"

He shook his head ruefully. "No."

"Do you have a very large staff?"

"Large enough. They're all very capable and do their jobs well." Taking the rod back from Amira, he asked Jared, "Ready to see if those fish are biting?"

The boy grinned at him, and Amira could see Jared was having a terrifically good time.

The morning passed pleasantly and swiftly as Amira sat with Jared and Brent, watching them fish. Jared was fascinated by everything—the boat and how it ran, the fishing rod, the type of fish in the lake. The breeze tossed Amira's hair. It was nippy with the sun still dancing behind the clouds, and she shivered.

Brent must have noticed. He unzipped his jacket, shrugged out of it and put it around her shoulders.

"I can't take this. You'll get cold."

He was wearing a sweatshirt with his jeans, and he shook his head. "I'm fine. My sweatshirt is heavier than your sweater."

Brent's jacket carried his warmth as well as his scent. She liked being wrapped up in both.

"If you get too cold, we'll go back."

Seeing the disappointment in Jared's eyes, she quickly shook her head. "I can always sit inside. I'm not going to spoil this fishing trip."

Brent's gaze was approving as he reached over and took her hand and warmed it under his. Sitting here with him and Jared, Amira could imagine a similar day with her own children. As she thought about being pregnant with Brent's child, a sense of pride and well-being blossomed inside of her.

Could she give up her life in Penwyck if he asked her to? It was all she'd ever known. Still, a future with Brent was becoming her heart's desire.

You can't base your future on knowing a man for only a week, her better sense told her.

Yet she felt she knew Brent in every way that mattered.

Nevertheless, if all Brent felt was desire, what did they have to build on?

Throughout the morning Amira looked for signs that Brent felt more than physical attraction. She thought she saw a few. He was kind to her, cared about her comfort and seemed to enjoy being with her. But love consisted of a lot more than caring.

It was almost four when Brent piloted the pontoon boat back to the dock and tied it down. He swung the almost-empty picnic basket as he took Amira's hand and Jared ran ahead of them. They were about twenty yards from the house when the back door opened. A girl of about eight stepped outside. She had long brown hair tied in pigtails and a wide smile on her face.

Jared took off with a loud whoop, and moments later he was on the porch hugging his sister.

Tears sprang to Amira's eyes as she and Brent stopped and watched. "I can see why you put your time and heart into Reunion House," she murmured.

"I remember the reunion my brother and I had after being separated for nine months. Even though I knew we'd be separated again eventually, that first moment was pure hope and happiness and everything we'd ever meant to each other."

Brent's barriers were down and Amira felt honored that she could share this moment with him. He was a man who could love deeply. The question was—would he let himself love her?

Brent must have felt the closeness between them, too, because he draped his arm around her shoulders and they walked up the path to Reunion House together.

They only stayed at the house long enough to meet Lena and see that she and Jared, as well as the other kids, were well occupied. Cocoa seemed to be at home there already and thoroughly satisfied with her new environment.

When Brent pulled into the drive at Shady Glenn, there was already a car there.

"Quentin's early," Brent said brusquely as he unfastened his seat belt.

After Brent came around and opened Amira's door for her, they approached the porch. A man had been sitting in one of the cane rockers and rose to greet them. He was about five-eight, stocky, with brown hair. His suit and tie seemed out of place here.

As Amira smiled at him, she thought he looked familiar. Had she seen him somewhere before, or did he simply look like somebody she might know?

On the porch Brent introduced Amira to the man. "Quentin Franklin, Amira Corbin."

She shook his hand still trying to place him. Where had she seen Quentin Franklin before?

# Chapter Nine

As Marcus sipped from his first cup of coffee for the day, he heard the shower running upstairs. Last evening had been one of the most frustrating of his life, but one of the most satisfying. It had been frustrating because he'd been close enough to Amira to kiss her as they'd sat on the sofa in front of the fire and played Scrabble. It had been satisfying because she was quick and bright and funny and had not only played the game, but talked and teased and laughed, too. He couldn't remember ever being that relaxed with a woman—comfortable enough to take off his shoes and not worry about what he should say or do or be. He could just be himself.

Only…she didn't know who he really was.

The phone rang and he automatically picked it up. "Hello?"

"I'd like to speak to Amira Corbin."

Now Marcus checked the Caller ID and saw the international code. "I'm sorry. She's not available right now. Can I give her a message?'' he asked smoothly as if he was a clerk at a desk.

There was silence and then he heard, ''This is Queen Marissa of Penwyck.''

This was the woman who might want to place the responsibility for a country on his head. ''Hello, Queen Marissa. What would you like me to tell Miss Corbin?''

''Do you know when she will be available?''

All he wanted to do was get the woman off the phone. Thinking about how long it usually took Amira to dress, he answered, ''She'll be here for breakfast in about half an hour.''

''I imagine she's taking her early-morning jog?''

''I don't think she ran today, but I'm certain she'll be here for breakfast in a half hour.''

''All right. Please tell her to call me immediately.''

''I'll do that. It was an honor to speak with you, Your Majesty.''

When Marcus hung up the receiver, he felt relieved but unsettled, too. That had been the woman who thought she might be his birth mother.

Twenty minutes later Amira came into the kitchen looking beautifully fresh and casual in jeans and a sweater. She was wearing her new shoes and had her hair tied back in a ponytail.

He poured a cup of coffee for her and set it on the table. ''You had a phone call.''

Amira lost her relaxed look and asked, ''Who was it?''

''It was the queen.''

Her eyes widened. ''Why didn't you come and get me?''

''Because you were in the shower.''

"That doesn't matter. If the queen wanted me—"

He felt impatient with her and the whole impossible situation. "Don't be ridiculous, Amira. What would you have done? Answered the phone dripping wet?"

"Yes!"

Immersed in the vision of her answering the phone that way, he shook his head. "I didn't think a few minutes would make a difference. In fact, you could probably eat breakfast first and the world won't fall apart." He was frustrated by her royal connection, knowing what it could mean to his life. He could also feel the sand in their hourglass running out, and not seeing her again disturbed him more than he wanted to admit.

"What did she say?" Amira asked, her voice strained.

"She said to call her immediately."

Amira went to the phone and asked coolly, "May I have a bit of privacy?"

"Fine," he said, exasperated with her. "I'll be in my office."

As Amira blinked away tears, she was angry with Brent for dismissing the call as if Queen Marissa had been a phone solicitor. She'd seen the exasperation and frustration in his eyes and knew full well what it was from. When he'd given her a good-night kiss last night, it had been a question. She'd ended the kiss before she'd been swept away again, and he'd left her at her bedroom door, wanting him.

Trying to push her relationship with Brent to the back of her mind, she dialed the queen's number. Her secretary, Mrs. Ferth, answered and then she transferred the call to the queen.

"Amira?"

"Yes, Queen Marissa. Has something happened?"

"Indeed it has. Prince Dylan has finally returned home. He's been traveling through remote areas of Europe. That's why we couldn't reach him."

"But he's home now?"

"Yes. He made a stop in Paris and heard about the king's health, Megan's pregnancy and marriage, Owen's kidnapping and return. He was very surprised his brother has a child and that Owen actually got down on his knees to ask Jordan to marry him."

Everyone had been surprised at that! "Had Dylan heard about Princess Anastasia's plane crash?"

"No, he hadn't. But he's pleased to see her with Jake Sanderstone. He thinks Jake can keep her in line. His words—not mine."

"Does he know about…?" Amira didn't know how to put the mix-up with the royal twins delicately.

"Does he know he might not be the true prince?" Queen Marissa formed the question for her. "Yes. I told him what Broderick says he did and how I tried to foil his machinations. But Dylan doesn't seem too concerned. He has always felt Owen outshone him in everything and assumed his brother would eventually be named king. That's why he took off on this trip of his in the first place. So the idea that Marcus and Shane Cordello might be the true heirs doesn't faze him. He was more disconcerted by the possibility that King Morgan and I might not be his parents. As with Owen, I assured both of my sons that I will always be their mother no matter what DNA reveals."

Amira felt compassion for the queen and the whole situation. She had worried in silence about Dylan while he was gone. "I'm so glad Dylan's home and that you can stop worrying about him."

"I'll always worry about my children. Dylan did say he'll help us any way he can to get to the bottom of Broderick's plot. I think he's quite eager to meet Marcus Cordello himself."

"I'll do everything in my power to speak to Marcus Cordello when he returns to the city. I'll be on his office doorstep Monday morning ready to confront him. Somehow I'll get through those doors into his office. I will not let my country down."

"We know you'll do your very best, my dear. Are you finding your accommodations suitable where you're staying?"

Amira looked around the kitchen and into the living room. She was very comfortable here. "It's very casual, Your Majesty, but very peaceful, too."

"None of us have had much of that lately. You get your fill of peace and quiet while you can and enjoy yourself."

After Amira hung up the phone, she knew she had to get something straight with Brent and get it straight now.

She found him at his large mahogany desk, his laptop computer switched on. When he heard her, he swiveled toward her. "Well? Is the country still in one piece?"

"You can make fun of me if you like," she said coolly. "But if I receive another call from the queen, please let me know immediately. A subject should never keep Her Majesty waiting."

Brent stood, his eyes stormy. "No one is that important that you can't take a breath before you return their call. You act as if she owns you."

Amira's feelings for Brent, somewhere between a hope and a dream, brought tears to her eyes. "You'll never understand my duties, my world…my life.'' Spinning around, she headed for the kitchen and went outside, not knowing where she was going. She just knew she didn't want this idyll with Brent to end. She didn't want to go back to her duties, her world and her life, but yet she had to. She had no choice. Penwyck was where she belonged. Brent would never understand that…never understand what her life was.

She took off at a run when she left the house, and before she realized it, she'd followed a path through birches and elms and found herself at the edge of the lake.

Brent caught up to her as she stood on the bank edged with laurel, staring at the pontoon boat a quarter of the way around the lake.

She could hear his feet rustling the leaves as he came up behind her. ''Help me understand the world you come from.''

When she turned to face him, he was hardly a breath away. She could see his annoyance with her was gone now.

''I *don't* understand, Amira,'' he said gently. ''But I'd like to.''

The intensity in his eyes was more than she could handle at the moment, and she looked away. ''It's difficult to explain.''

Tenderly, so very tenderly, he cupped her face in his hand. ''You don't run away from 'difficult.' I know that about you.''

No, she didn't. So she tried to do as he asked. ''On Penwyck, everything revolves around the royal family. They can hardly take a walk without newspapers wanting to cover them. Although my father was part of the Royal Guard, he never talked about the family.

In his silence I sensed his loyalty, the attitude of discretion everyone around him followed. My father was a wonderful man—kind and gentle, yet strong and sure. I was always so proud of him when I saw him protecting the king. That's what I remember most—how he stood, handsome in his uniform, flanking the king wherever he went."

"Like our Secret Service," Brent responded.

"Yes, exactly like that. I always knew that if he had to my father would give his life for King Morgan. But I never believed that would happen. When I was a child I saw the palace as a fairy-tale castle and believed nothing bad could happen in King Morgan and Queen Marissa's kingdom. Then in one terrible night I learned I was all wrong."

"You learned about real life."

Amira realized that just as her father's death was a life-changing event for her, Brent had had a similar one when his parents divorced and he was separated from his brother. "I learned about reality," she agreed, "but I also learned about loyalty and kindness. The royal family took in my mother and me and gave us new lives. The queen invited my mother to become her lady-in-waiting. My mother became her confidante. Queen Marissa arranged for private tutors for me, and Princess Anastasia, especially, became like a big sister to me. Princess Meredith and Princess Megan were older, but they never acted as if they resented me. Neither did Prince Dylan or Prince Owen. It was as if the queen and king had decreed us part of the family, and all of them appreciated the sacrifice my father had made. Because of him, the king lived. Because of him, Penwyck still had its monarch."

"I'm beginning to understand," Brent said, and she could see from his expression that he was.

"They gave me my life. After my schooling was finished, Queen Marissa found a place for me in the academy. Everything at Penwyck is about loyalty and honor."

"So it's natural for you to be on call, to fly to the United States to meet a man who's a stranger, to return a phone call immediately. Tell me something, Amira. Do you like your life?"

Again she felt she had to be honest. "Before I came here I thought about getting my own apartment but not changing my life. Now...I don't know. Sometimes all of it is a burden, and sometimes it gives my life meaning."

"I could never live like you do. Never."

"Most people can't," she admitted, thinking about a life here with Brent. But he didn't want to share his life on an ongoing basis. No matter what she did or what she changed, that wouldn't change.

Brent's cell phone beeped and he glanced at it askance. "I'm supposed to be on vacation," he muttered, taking it from his belt and slipping it open. "Yes?" he asked tersely.

Amira watched his face go grim. Taking her hand he started tugging her toward the house, and she hurried along beside him, worried.

She heard him say, "We're headed for the car now. We'll be there in two minutes." Snapping the phone shut, he clipped it back on his belt, not slowing his stride.

"What is it?"

"That was Marilyn. She can't find Jared and Lena anywhere. Apparently Lena's foster mother and father are getting a divorce. No one knows where Lena will be placed. Both kids are terrifically upset. I think Jared's afraid they'll ship her even farther away.''

''Where do you think they'd go?''

''He might take her to the woods with him, or he might hide out somewhere for a while. I just don't know. I *do* know ten-year-olds don't usually plan ahead.''

When Brent and Amira arrived at Reunion House, they searched it again with Joanie and Marilyn.

''We're wasting our time,'' Brent said as they stood in the foyer once more. ''He wouldn't take the chance of us finding them here. I'm going to the woods. Marilyn, call Emergency Services, and tell them we need to find these kids.''

''I'm going with you.'' Amira ran beside Brent as they hurried to the kitchen and out the back door into the yard.

Brent had his eyes peeled to the woods as they ran toward them. Suddenly he pointed. ''There. Did you see a flash of yellow?''

Amira had missed whatever Brent had seen. ''No, I didn't, but that doesn't mean it wasn't there.''

As they met the tree line, Brent tugged her along it. ''There. I saw it again. I think he's headed for the dock.''

Lena and Jared were a good hundred yards ahead. All Amira could make out were colors. One was definitely moving slower than the other. ''She's not running as fast as he is. Maybe she's hurt.''

''That's what I meant about kids not planning. I don't know what he thinks he's going to do on the dock. Unless—'' Brent swore and Amira guessed what Brent was imagining.

"I showed him how to do it," Brent muttered. "I showed him where I keep the key. Damn."

They heard the pontoon boat's engine start when they were still fifty yards from the dock. Brent surged ahead of her. "Wait on the dock for me."

"What are you going to do?"

"Go after them," he called over his shoulder, and she suddenly realized exactly what he intended. Her heart almost stopped.

The pontoon boat was chugging fast and picking up speed.

Afraid for Brent, Amira watched as he hopped on the Jet Ski and started it. She thought about his shoulder, about the wound that wasn't yet healed. What did he think he was going to do? He certainly couldn't stop the pontoon boat with a Jet Ski, could he?

Watching in fear and dismay, she saw him race on the surface of the lake, speeding so he could catch up with the boat. He looked as if he were flying. As he pulled up beside the pontoon boat, she saw with dread what he was going to do. He was going to jump onto the deck! What if he didn't make it? What if he fell between the two vehicles? Good Lord, she loved this man and she wanted nothing more than to spend the rest of her life with him. There was no doubt in her mind.

With bated breath, she saw Brent jump to the pontoon boat's deck, teeter for a moment, then leap over the rail. She had never been so relieved, never been so grateful. But what had it cost him? What if he had torn his shoulder open again?

Waiting on the dock was the hardest thing she'd

ever done as the Jet Ski skipped over the water until it hit the shore then fell on its side. In the meantime, Brent piloted the boat back to the dock. As soon as she could, she caught the line and helped him tie it up, noting Jared's and Lena's expressions. Lena looked scared, but Jared looked defiant.

Brent pointed toward the dock. "Out," he said gravely.

Jared hopped onto the dock first, and then Brent put his hands around Lena's waist and carried her to Amira. "She turned her ankle. Thank goodness or they would have been across the lake before we could catch them."

Jared turned on Brent then. "You shouldn't have brought us back. We're just going to run away again. You wait and see."

"If I hadn't caught you, where would you have gone? The lake is about three miles round. You wouldn't have gotten very far. What would you have done for shelter tonight. And food?"

The ten-year-old produced four cookies from his pocket. "We had food."

Brent shook his head and took Jared by the shoulders. "Running away is not going to solve anything."

"It'll keep us together," he almost shouted, his voice trembling between anger and tears. "I don't want them putting Lena somewhere where I can't call her, where I can't see her. We want to be together, Mr. Carpenter. Please."

Amira's heart went out to the two children, and she knew Brent's did, too.

Crouching down in front of Jared, Brent studied the boy for a long time, then he looked at Lena. "I can't make you any promises, but I do know people in the system. Let me see what I can do.''

"You mean we'll be together?" Jared asked, wariness in his tone.

"I'll try to make that happen. Can you trust that I'll do my best for you?''

Jared and Lena exchanged a look. "I guess we can't stay at a motel without a credit card.''

The corner of Brent's mouth turned up. "Not unless you have a bunch of cash.''

"Don't have much, just five dollars from chores.''

It seemed to take a very long time for Jared to decide what he was going to do. "All right. We'll give you a chance.''

Brent extended his hand to the boy. "Shake on it?''

Jared put his hand into Brent's, and Amira felt her throat constrict. The brother and sister had such hope in their eyes, such trust in Brent's power to reunite them. What if she trusted Brent, too? What if she trusted what she felt and gave in to it?

After Brent called the dispatcher to let them know Jared and Lena had been found, he sat down with the brother and sister and Marilyn again, getting specific information from them so he could make a few calls.

Amira tended to Lena's ankle, putting an ice pack on it and propping it on a stool. Although she kept close to Jared, Lena's eyes were filled with a thank-you, and when it was time for Brent and Amira to go back to Shady Glenn, Lena waved to her. Amira felt as if she'd made a friend.

Thinking about everything that had happened, Amira was quiet on the drive back to Shady Glenn. When Brent pulled up in front of the house, he didn't cut the engine. "I'm going to go around the lake and see about that Jet Ski."

"You're not serious."

"Of course I am." He studied her carefully. "What's the matter?"

"I was worried about you. I still am. You should let me check your shoulder."

"I'll tell you what. Why don't you go in and make us some hot chocolate. I'll make sure the ski didn't damage anyone's property and I'll be right back. Promise."

"You'll be right back?"

"Fifteen minutes tops."

She didn't want to act like a meddling fussbudget. "Okay. I'll put something together for us for lunch."

As Brent drove off, Amira went inside and fixed a tray of sandwiches, covered them and set them in the refrigerator. True to his word, he returned fifteen minutes later. When he took off his jacket, she noticed the nerve in his jaw working. That meant he was in pain.

"The gauze patches and tape are upstairs. Let's go tend to your shoulder."

"You have a one-track mind," he said with patient amusement.

If he only knew what track her mind was on.

As they mounted the steps, she could feel his gaze on her. At the top of the stairs he asked, "Bathroom or my bedroom?"

"This will be easier if you're sitting on the bed." She remembered the last time she had done this and how she had left him afterward. She could see he was remembering, too.

As she'd done before, she stood between his legs to change the bandage. But this time something was different. This time she wasn't denying everything she was feeling. This time she secured the last piece of tape and then looked into his eyes.

"You scared me to death on the dock. I was afraid...I was afraid something terrible would happen to you."

He didn't make light of what she'd felt. Rather he took her hands in his. "I didn't know what was going to happen out there. I just knew I had to get on that boat and stop them before they hurt themselves."

"You're a hero," she said, her admiration obvious.

"Oh, Amira..." He shook his head. "I'm not a hero. I just did what I had to do." He lifted her fingers to his lips and kissed them one by one.

She never knew her fingertips were connected to her heart. She never knew her heart could feel so full or so sad at the same time. "We only have a few days left," she murmured.

His green gaze was questioning as he raised his head. "I know. What would you like to do with those days?"

"It doesn't matter...as long as I'm with you."

Releasing her hands, he slid his arms around her and brought her closer. "I want you," he said, his voice deep with need.

"I want you, too," she whispered.

"Are you sure?" he asked, and she knew if she hesitated at all, he would restrain himself and pull away.

Remembering how she'd felt on that dock, thinking about everything she'd learned about him over the past week, how she was going to feel leaving him when she returned to Penwyck, she said boldly, "I'm sure."

Brent tugged her down onto his lap then and kissed her as if he'd never kissed her before and would never kiss her again. Parting her lips, he ravished her mouth with the inflamed desire of a man who had waited too long. When she moaned softly, overwhelmed by the sensuality of the kiss, she wanted to give him everything she was.

Breaking away, he took a deep breath. "I want to do this slowly, Amira. I want you to know the full pleasure of everything a man and a woman can do for each other."

"We don't have to go slow." She had read books about what was going to happen, but her first time with Brent couldn't be found in any book. "I trust you," she said simply.

He kissed her again and eased her back onto the bed. "This is going to be good, Amira. I promise you that."

She wasn't exactly sure how he defined *good,* but as soon as he trailed kisses across her mouth, down her chin and throat into the vee of her sweater, she was trembling. While his mouth worked its magic, his hands slid under her sweater and pushed it up. His skin on hers was hot, taunting, so deliciously erotic that she couldn't help but move restlessly so he would touch more.

"Easy," he said to her, "let's take this off." With slow care he lifted her sweater over her head, admired her breasts in the lacy bra, and then he was unfastening it, touching her, putting his lips to her nipple.

She'd never felt anything so exquisite, and she cried his name.

His hand went to her jeans. "It's going to get even better, sweetheart. I promise."

He was about to unfasten her zipper when his hand stilled.

At first she was so caught up in what was happening between them she barely noticed. But then he shifted and sat up, and she felt bereft without him covering her. "What is it?"

"I heard something downstairs—"

"Is anybody home?" came a deep male voice at the foot of the stairs.

Amira plucked up her sweater and held it in front of her breasts. "Oh, my gosh. Is it Fritz?"

"No, it's not Fritz. It's my father. I'd better get down there before he comes up here."

Sliding off the bed and pushing himself to his feet, Brent took a deep breath. Then he bent down to her, kissed her hard on the lips and assured her, "You'll like Dad and he'll like you. Tonight after he goes to bed, we'll finish where we left off."

As Brent went into the hall and called down to his dad, Amira couldn't wait for tonight to come. She loved Brent Carpenter and she was going to show him exactly how much.

# Chapter Ten

Glancing outside the kitchen window, Amira saw Brent and his dad deep in conversation while Brent cooked the hamburgers on the outdoor grill. She liked his father very much. He'd immediately told her to call him Joe, and his hazel eyes had been friendly. She'd been embarrassed a little while ago when she'd descended the steps and her gaze had met Brent's. But his smile had been as intimate as before. It told her he wanted to be with her as much as she wanted to be with him.

As she mixed an olive oil and lemon juice dressing for a pasta salad that Owen's wife Jordan had taught her how to make, she thought about the night to come. She wanted to know Brent in every way, and she wanted him to know her. Maybe tonight she could tell him how she felt. Maybe tonight she could tell him she wanted to see him again after she returned to Penwyck. Maybe tonight they could talk about her moving to the United States permanently. It would be a risk for her, but it would be worth it if Brent could come to love her. Maybe the idea was altogether fool-hardy, but she was tired of living a protected existence.

When the phone rang, she thought about letting the machine pick it up, but then the Caller ID showed the number that Cole Everson had used.

The head of the Royal Intelligence Institute got straight to the point. "I have a picture, Amira. I'm going to fax it to you as soon as we finish here. I also have Cordello's home address. Watching the post office box didn't work. No one picked up the mail after I began surveillance. It was as if he knew we were watching. But we found a deed for a purchase of a house near De Kalb and that gave us his home address in the paperwork. I'll also fax that information to you."

"A house near De Kalb?" At first a frisson of fore-boding skipped down her spine. But then she told herself she was being silly. Lots of inhabitants of Chicago must have houses in the state and maybe De Kalb was a popular area.

"With this information," Cole went on, "you'll know who you're looking for and have a second place to look. But the queen doesn't expect you to take on the role of a private investigator. If you still can't corner the man after a few days, I'll bring in a pro-fessional. As soon as we hang up, I'll fax you what I have. Good luck, Amira."

When Amira hung up the phone, she no longer gave a second thought to the dressing for the pasta salad or to the frozen vegetables on the counter. Rather she went to Brent's study to wait for the faxes.

\* \* \*

The aroma of hamburgers wafted into the fall air as Marcus stared at his father in astonishment. "Shane and I are adopted?"

Joseph Cordello had gone along with his son's wishes to call him Brent when he'd arrived at Shady Glenn. But as soon as they stepped outside and had a bit of privacy, he wanted to know why. Marcus had filled him in, giving him the tale Amira had related, adding the rest of what she had told him about life on Penwyck. Then his father had revealed the secret he'd been keeping for twenty-three years.

Joseph's eyes were anguished. "I never wanted you to find out like this. So suddenly."

"Suddenly? Dad, I'm twenty-three years old!" Marcus was feeling more than shock now. Anger mixed with it. His world had just been rocked again by his father's revelation.

Joseph Cordello took a deep breath but kept his gaze steady on his son's. "When your mother and I divorced, we felt you were too young. We decided to wait until you and Shane were eighteen. But the time never seemed right. We wanted to tell you and Shane together, but the four of us were rarely in the same state…"

Although Marcus was keeping a tight rein on all of his emotions, his turmoil must have shown because his father stopped then and said, "You have every right to be angry. But we didn't tell you because we love you both. In every way that matters, we *are* your parents."

Unable to watch the pained look in his dad's eyes, Marcus took a few steps away from the grill and looked toward the lake. "Who *are* our birth parents?"

His dad answered quickly. "According to our lawyer, they were a young couple who were in a terrible accident. They both perished. An aunt was baby-sitting you and Shane at the time.''

''Why didn't the aunt take us?''

''She was elderly and knew she couldn't handle bringing up twins. She also didn't want to separate you. She wanted a good family to raise you.''

Marcus swung around and faced his father again. ''Did you ever meet the aunt?''

''No. No, we didn't. We were told traveling was difficult for her. Our lawyer and his wife transferred you to us.''

The full realization of everything his father had told him hit him. ''Then Amira's story *could* be true.''

Since his father had arrived and Marcus had had to leave Amira in his bed, he'd thought only of her and what they'd been about to do. As he'd introduced her to his father, he'd decided he couldn't make love to her without telling her who he was. He'd decided to ask her to help him keep the world outside at bay with him until Monday.

Now he had to tell her the truth not only to restore real honesty to their relationship but because he might very well be one of the Penwyck heirs!

As he heard the back door open, he turned and saw Amira coming down the steps with her head bowed. It was crazy, but he always missed her when they were apart, even if it wasn't for very long. In the midst of all that he'd learned, honesty between them became the priority. Deciding supper would have to wait until he revealed the truth to her, he became aware of the papers in her hand.

She raised her face to him, and he didn't have to ask her what they were. He knew.

He'd decided to tell her the truth hoping nothing would change between them. That had been optimism at its worst. Her wounded expression tore at his heart and the look of betrayal in her eyes lanced his soul.

"Why did you do it?" she asked, her voice rising as she shook the papers at him. "Why did you tell me you were somebody else?"

He stepped closer to her, but she backed away and he stilled. "I didn't intend for it to go this far. Let me explain."

"Explain? There *are* no explanations. You're Marcus Cordello! I poured my heart out to you. I told you how much I needed to see him and why. You sat there and listened, being sympathetic, learning how much it mattered to me and everyone at Penwyck. And still you didn't say a word. You deceived me all this time, playing with my emotions, leading me on. I can't believe I wasn't intelligent enough to put it all together. I met you in the hotel where your offices are. Your secretary's name is Barbra. How could I have let that pass?"

For the time being, he buried his feelings about his father's revelation and concentrated on Amira. "You let it pass for the same reason I couldn't tell you the truth. We were getting to know each other and nothing else mattered."

"My mission mattered."

He could see the tears glistening in her eyes as the strength of her emotions shook her voice. "Amira..."

"The first time we saw your doorman," she went on, "you cut him off. He was going to call you by your real name. And that man who came here yesterday...I knew I'd seen him somewhere before. One of those days I was sitting outside your office, he came out. You've played me for an utter fool. This afternoon I thought—'' Her cheeks grew red, her lower lip trembled, and Marcus had never felt so low in his life.

"It's not the way you think."

"It's *exactly* the way I think. You saw me as some shy little twit who didn't know the first thing about men. You thought you could take advantage of me—''

Marcus knew he had no defense. But he *had* struggled with becoming involved with her because of who he was and where she was from, and the fact that she was shy and innocent. "I never took advantage of you."

"What about this afternoon? If your father hadn't arrived, you wouldn't have stopped."

Suddenly uncomfortable with having this discussion in front of his father, Marcus knew it was where they had to have it because Amira would never let him talk with her about this calmly inside. Still he had to give it a try. "Let's go inside and discuss this."

"I'm not going anywhere with you."

That's the response he'd expected. "This afternoon, Amira, we were both in that bed. Neither one of us would have put a stop to it if my father hadn't arrived. You might be shy sometimes and you *are* innocent, but you're your own woman, too. You made the decision to be with me."

Her gaze darted to his father and, as she realized they were discussing their most private matters in front of him, she looked thoroughly mortified.

Marcus wished he could put his arms around her, persuade her to believe that his father wouldn't judge anything. But he knew she wouldn't let him get close to her. He knew she'd never let him touch her again.

Although her eyes glistened with unshed tears, she squared her shoulders. "I'm leaving here tonight. When I get back to the city, I'm taking the first flight out. Someone from Penwyck will be in touch with you. I hope you don't play the same games with them that you played with me." Then she turned and practically ran into the house.

Marcus didn't think he had ever heard a more earth-shattering silence. As the door slammed, he started to go after her, but his father put a restraining hand on his shoulder. "I don't think another confrontation is a good idea."

"I can't let her leave like this."

"I think you're going to have to. In the state she's in, you set a foot near her, and she's going to *walk* back to Chicago. I'll offer her my driver. He's at a motel in De Kalb. He can be here in half an hour."

"I can't let her leave," Marcus said again.

"If you don't let her leave, you might never get her back. *If* that's what you want. I think you'd better be sure exactly what you want before you talk to her again."

Marcus took a long look at Joseph Cordello, remembering the man wasn't his biological father. Yet, hearing his advice, Marcus felt his anger at being kept in the dark for twenty-three years vanish. This man was his "real" father in every definition of the word. "All right. Offer her your driver."

As Joseph Cordello went inside, Marcus felt as if the foundation of his life had cracked in two and nothing would ever be the same again.

\* \* \*

The Jet Ski skimmed the surface of the lake, but Marcus got no pleasure from the speed. He'd felt turned inside out since Amira had left. Making repairs at Reunion House hadn't helped. Taking long drives hadn't helped. Assembling the jungle gym hadn't helped. Running until he'd dropped hadn't helped. Talking to his dad hadn't helped. No matter what he did, he thought about her, about who she was, about who they could be together.

The day after Amira had left he'd tried to put her out of his mind by having a talk with Jared's foster mother and dad and then the authorities. The family who had taken Jared in would also take Lena. They'd been unable to do that a year ago, but since then they'd moved to a larger house and Mr. Brinkman had gotten a promotion. The satisfaction in what he'd been able to do had come when Jared hugged him. Even then all he could think about was having children of his own with Amira as their mother.

He gave the Jet Ski more power, seeking to outrun the pain and the feeling of emptiness. But he couldn't outrun it, and he knew he should stop trying.

When he returned to the dock, his father was standing there waiting for him. His dad had come along to Reunion House this morning to help him with the jungle gym. "You had a call," Joseph said.

"Amira?" he asked, knowing that was improbable but hoping nonetheless.

His father shook his head. "Sorry, no. It was a Mrs. Dunlap, Cocoa's owner. Apparently she called Barbra and Barbra gave her the number here. She phoned a veterinarian, who told her that you found Cocoa. Only her name isn't Cocoa, it's Brownie. I told her where you'd taken Brownie and how much the kids loved her. She said her arthritis is getting worse and she can't walk Brownie as much as she'd like. Brownie slipped her collar one day when they went for a walk. I think Mrs. Dunlap would like to visit Reunion House and see if the dog really has a good home. If she does, she'd like to visit now and then.''

"That would be a good solution for everyone," Marcus said. "I'll have Fritz drive her up here as soon as I get back to the city."

"Are you going back tomorrow?"

Tomorrow was Sunday. He'd promised to have dinner with Marilyn and the kids before he left. "Fritz will arrive in the late afternoon, and we'll start back then. What about you?"

"I'll leave first thing in the morning." He paused, then asked, "Are we all right, Marcus? Can you still think of me as your father?"

Having a few days to let it all sink in had helped. He realized his dad was the same man he'd always known, and he still felt admiration, respect and love for him. "We're all right, Dad. I could never think of anyone else as my father."

His dad capped Marcus's shoulder, and there was moisture in his eyes. He cleared his throat. "Are you going to tell Shane?"

"I have to decide the best way to do that."

"I'm surprised you haven't received a call from Penwyck."

"I don't even know if Amira flew back yet. Maybe she stayed. Maybe she'll be at my office bright and early Monday morning to meet me in an official capacity." His heart lifted at the thought.

"Do you really think that's likely?" His dad made him face the impracticality of that possibility.

In his mind's eye he could see Amira waiting for him at Shady Glenn, holding their child in her arms. "No, it's not likely."

"You know, son, I was a fool where your mother was concerned. We had problems, and I thought I wanted more than she could give me. I made a terrible mistake that she could never forgive. But I also didn't try very hard to win her forgiveness. My pride kept me from telling her that I still loved her. If Amira is the woman you want or need, don't let her simply fly away."

"She'll never forgive me."

"You don't know that, do you?"

No, he didn't know that. His mother hadn't been able to forgive, but maybe Amira could.

Suddenly Marcus realized he didn't just want to ask Amira for forgiveness because that was the right thing to do. He wanted her to forgive him because he loved her. He hadn't wanted to fall in love. He'd fought against it from the moment he'd met her. Her heart called to his and now he wanted to answer that call. He just hoped it wasn't too late. He just hoped he could convince her not only to forgive him but to trust him for the rest of their lives.

Filled with resolve, he said, "I'm going to ask Marilyn if I can change our dinner plans to tonight. Then I'm going to make reservations and see when I can get a flight out."

"This is serious, then," Joseph remarked as he and Marcus started walking toward Reunion House.

"This is it, Dad. The real thing. I found a woman I can't do without. Now I just have to convince her she can't do without me."

After discovering Amira had checked out of the

hotel, Marcus also found out that she'd made flight arrangements through the concierge and returned to Penwyck. Throughout Saturday night, he went over persuasive arguments in his mind. None seemed right, none seemed good enough. In spite of that, he got an early flight out the next morning.

Fortunately, he had time to stop in a jewelry store in the airport before he left.

His flight landed on schedule. Due to the time change, it was early evening when he arrived at the palace. As his taxi pulled up, he saw a gray limestone edifice three stories tall. Actually it looked like two buildings joined by a covered glassed-in walkway that was illuminated from the curved ceiling inside.

At the main entrance he gave his name to the guard, who called someone in the palace. Another guard dressed in the same red jacket and black slacks with a red beret escorted him through a garden to the covered hallway. The floor was marble as were the columns. There were floor-to-ceiling arched windows.

When they exited the walkway, they came to another long hall. Finally they stood before a large door. The guard opened it and Marcus stepped inside.

Marcus barely noticed the hand-carved plaster and gilded wainscoting, the marble fireplace with columns, the cream velvet sofa, the chairs covered in silk damask. The walls were decorated with paintings, water lilies by Monet, a Renoir, and a large photograph of what Marcus supposed was the royal family with their horses. Amira wasn't in the picture so he didn't stare at it very long. He glanced at the desk and saw no one was seated there.

Suddenly a door opened and two women walked in. The first woman looked to be in her forties. Her blond hair was pulled into a chignon at her nape similar to the way Amira had worn her hair the first night he'd met her. She had blue eyes that were very serious. The second woman was older, in her fifties. Her hair was dark and she wore it in a corona on the top of her head. She, too, had blue eyes and was strikingly beautiful. Her maroon silk blouse and tailored wool slacks suited her understated elegance.

The guard bowed and said formally, "Her Majesty, the Queen, and her lady-in-waiting, Gwendolyn Montague."

Marcus had asked to see the queen or Amira's mother, not knowing if an audience was that easily obtained. Apparently his name had carried some weight. Maybe a very lead weight.

Still, he bowed to the queen. "I'm honored." Then to Mrs. Montague, he said, "It's a pleasure to meet you, too."

Neither woman spoke so he addressed the situation immediately. "I've come for two reasons. First and foremost, to find Amira and convince her I'm not the blackguard she thinks I am. Secondly, I came to find out if my brother and I might be royal heirs. I had no idea we were adopted until a few days ago, so I had put the idea out of my mind since Amira first told me about it because I didn't want any part of it. I didn't want my life disrupted." He looked squarely at Amira's mother. "But your daughter did disrupt my life quite completely, and when she left I realized it was empty without her."

The queen and Gwen Montague exchanged a look.

"Well, Mr. Cordello," the queen finally responded. "You've deflated our indignation on Amira's behalf.

I think we were both ready to roast you over hot coals.''

Marcus thought he saw a twinkle of amusement in the queen's eyes. ''I think Amira would like to do something much worse,'' he said with complete seriousness.

The queen motioned to the grouping of furniture.

Marcus waited until the women were seated, and then he sat on the edge of one of the silk damask chairs that was as uncomfortable as any chair could be. But there was no way to make this conversation comfortable, antique chair or not.

Gwen Montague looked him straight in the eye. ''You haven't known my daughter very long, Mr. Cordello. Am I supposed to believe you care deeply for her after less than two weeks?''

''Amira told me the story of how you and your first husband met at an embassy ball. She said you knew from the moment you looked into his eyes that he was the man you belonged with. It was that way with me and Amira, although I didn't want to admit it. There are a lot of reasons for that—reasons why I pushed her away at first.''

''I know this might seem a bit indelicate,'' Gwen told him, ''but Amira seems to think you were only interested in getting her into bed.''

The queen's brows arched, and a bit of a smile lurked at the corner of her mouth as she saw how uncomfortable Marcus was with discussing this with Amira's mother.

He deserved this grilling and met it with honesty. ''That was my intention. When I asked her to go to Shady Glenn with me, I knew we'd have a week to be together. But I also never tried to take advantage of your daughter, Mrs. Montague. If she's honest with you, I think she'll tell you that."

The queen's lady-in-waiting paused for a moment. "She did tell me that, but I needed your explanation before I decided if she'd had the wool pulled over her eyes or not."

"I imagine you'll have to get to know me before you can make any decisions about my character and my feelings for your daughter. But I am going to ask her to marry me."

Again the queen and Amira's mother exchanged a look.

"Amira's still quite upset," the queen interjected. "She's changed since her trip to the United States. She's talking about moving out of the palace, living on her own. If you're not the prince, as you hope you're not, your life in Chicago will remain as it has always been. Would you expect Amira to give up everything she knows here?"

"I'm not sure what we'll do. We'll have to work it out...together."

"Mr. Cordello, I don't know what Gwen thinks, but I believe you're an honorable man. Since she's Amira's mother, though, it's up to her to decide whether or not she'll tell Amira that you've come."

"Is she here now?" he asked, determined to search every room in the palace for her if he had to.

Gwen Montague must have seen that determination in his eyes and maybe some of what he felt for Amira, too. "I have the feeling you'd tear the palace down to find her," she said, her voice a bit friendly now.

"I would. I know how special she is."

Silence reigned for a moment.

"All right, Mr. Cordello," Gwen Montague decided. "I'll tell you where you can find her. The rest is up to you. She's having dinner in town at the Artist's Place. It's a small café."

"Yes, she told me about it. They have new artists' work on display."

"Yes, it's one of her favorite spots to go when she wants to think. She just left about half an hour ago, so you should be able to catch her there. Do you need a driver?"

"I asked the cab to wait." He stood, not knowing if it was proper or not, but wanting to be on his way. "I'm glad I had the opportunity to meet both of you."

"We'll need to discuss DNA testing," the queen reminded him.

"Yes, I know we will. If you want to set something up, that's fine."

"Then you will stay at the palace tonight?" the queen asked.

"If that's what you'd like."

"That's what I'd like. No matter how things go with Amira. You might be the next heir, Mr. Cordello. You deserve to be here."

After he bowed to the queen, he shook Gwen Montague's hand. "Thank you for being open-minded."

"Amira's young but she knows her own mind. I wish you luck, Mr. Cordello."

"Marcus," he said automatically.

Gwen nodded. "Marcus."

The guard escorted Marcus out of the palace the same way he'd come in. As he descended the steps, he realized that these guards probably had stories to tell, but they never would. Their loyalty was obvious in their demeanor.

Marcus gave the cab driver the name of the restaurant and then he tried to organize his thoughts, tried to come up with the best arguments, tried to hope Amira wouldn't turn him away.

As the cab neared the center of Marleston, he couldn't help but remember his mother's inability to forgive his father. He remembered Amira saying when trust is broken it's hard to repair the damage. He'd broken her trust, and the damage had been great.

In front of the Artist's Place, he paid the driver and got out of the cab. He decided not to have the man wait. One way or another he'd get back to the palace.

He pulled open a heavy wooden door and stepped inside a dimly lit foyer. The place looked like a quiet pub. Artwork hung on all the walls and sculptures stood on pedestals. The heavy wooden tables were surrounded by black leather barrel chairs. There was a sign on the lectern before the archway that led into the restaurant: Please Seat Yourself. Apparently, Sunday nights were quiet ones here. Only four tables were occupied.

He spotted Amira immediately to the rear of the restaurant at a corner table where the light was the dimmest. Her blond hair reflected it. There was a sandwich before her, but she wasn't eating. She was just staring at the pictures on the walls. His heart hammered so hard he couldn't think. He could only feel.

He strode through the room quickly, coming to stand at Amira's table. "Lady Amira Sierra Corbin?" he asked formally.

At the sound of his voice, her chin came up and her astonishment was evident in her eyes.

"I'd like to introduce myself," he went on. "My name is Marcus Cordello, and I'm searching for the most incredible woman I've ever met. I did something foolish by not revealing to her who I really was as soon as I realized she was looking for me. Once the die was cast, I didn't know how to turn it around.''

Dropping the formality, he spoke from his heart. ''I wanted that week at Shady Glenn with you in case I never saw you again. But when you left, the idea of never seeing you again was intolerable.'' He went down on one knee beside her, ''I never meant to hurt you. I never meant to take advantage of you. I never meant to fall deeply in love with you, but I did.'' Dipping his hand into his pocket, he brought out the small black box. ''If you agree to marry me, I'll spend the rest of my life making up to you for my deception. I promise you I will never tell you anything that isn't true again. I love you, Amira. I can't imagine my life without your laughter, your sincerity, your compassion. Will you honor me by becoming my wife?''

Amira looked absolutely stunned. She stared down at the ring in the box. It was a large heart-shaped diamond with smaller diamonds swirled on either side. It was a ring fit for a princess…a ring fit for the woman he loved as much as life.

Finally she looked up at him with tears slipping down her cheeks. ''Marcus?''

''What, sweetheart?'' he asked gently.

''I was just trying out your name. It fits.''

His pulse was racing fast and hope seemed to overtake his whole heart. ''Can we see if the ring fits, too?''

Taking it out of the box, he slipped it onto her finger. Looking up at her again, he asked, ''Can you forgive me?''

''I forgive you, Marcus. I love you.'' And then she was in his arms. They were both standing, and he was kissing her with all the love and fervor and commitment that he couldn't give her before.

The kiss went on and on and on until there was applause from other patrons in the restaurant.

Marcus lifted his head, hoping Amira wasn't too embarrassed. "I should have done this privately," he murmured. But I couldn't wait."

"I'm glad you didn't wait," she managed shakily.

Pulling his chair close to hers, he sat down beside her, holding her hand. "Are you sure?"

"I'm sure. I know what kind of man you are."

He winced at that.

"Although, when I found out who you were," she continued, "I felt betrayed and disappointed and didn't know if anything we'd experienced was real. I didn't know how I was going to ever see you, look at you again, if you came here to get the prince dilemma straightened out. I had decided to fly to Paris and enroll in school there. But tonight, sitting here, I realized that would be running away, and I didn't want to run away from you. I was going to stay here until you came to Penwyck, and then I would find out if you felt anything for me or if my imagination had just gone wild."

She was beautiful and courageous...and his. "Your imagination didn't go wild. I began falling in love with you from that first night. Sure I felt desire and I wanted you in my bed. But I wanted so much more and didn't even realize it. As each day passed and I thought about you leaving, I grabbed on to whatever we could have."

"Before I left Shady Glenn, your father admitted he'd just told you that you were adopted. That must have been a shock. What will happen if you *are* the

prince?'' she asked, gazing down at her ring and looking back up at him. ''I know you don't want that. I
know—''

''The queen asked me what I'd do if I *wasn't* the
prince and you accepted my proposal. She wanted to
know if I expected you to turn your life upside down
for me. I don't have all the answers, Amira. I don't
know how I'll feel if I am the prince. But I do know
that I love you and that I want your happiness as
much as mine. I told her we'd work everything out
together.''

Amira's hand came up to his jaw then, and she
stroked it with her fingers. ''You're right. We'll work
everything out…together.''

Then, unmindful whether anyone else was watching or not, they kissed again. This time they weren't
interrupted by applause. This time the kiss went on
much longer until finally they both needed to come
up for air.

After their lips clung and they drew apart, Marcus
gave a wry shake of his head. ''How soon can we get
married?''

''A few weeks maybe?'' she asked.

''Is that enough time for you to plan a fairy-tale
wedding?'' He imagined that's what she would want,
and he could see from the light shining in her eyes
that he was right.

''My mother and the queen can do wonders. It will
be enough time.''

''Good. I don't think I could last more than a few
weeks without really making you mine.''

''You can do that tonight,'' she said from a new
boldness that came from a confidence in what they
were together.

But he shook his head. "No, I want to do this right. You'll be giving me a wonderful gift, and I want to give it the respect it deserves, the respect *you* deserve."

She threw her arms around his neck and tilted her forehead against his. "No matter what the DNA testing shows, you *are* a prince. You're my prince."

Marcus knew he would do everything in his power to live up to her faith in him. "I love you," he said again, wanting to make sure she knew it.

In a few weeks he would pledge his heart and soul and life to her and she to him. Whatever life brought, they'd face it together—hand in hand, heart in heart. They would love and cherish each other...forever.

\* \* \* \* \*

*Royal romance heats up as*

CROWN & GLORY

*moves into Silhouette Desire next month
with Maureen Child's*

*THE ROYAL TREATMENT.*

*A powerful earthquake ravages Southern California...*

*Thousands are trapped beneath the rubble...*

*The men and women of Morgan Trayhern's team face their most heroic mission yet...*

A brand-new series from
*USA TODAY* bestselling author

# LINDSAY McKENNA

Don't miss these breathtaking stories of the triumph of love!

Look for one title per month from each Silhouette series:

**August: THE HEART BENEATH**
(Silhouette Special Edition #1486)

**September: RIDE THE THUNDER**
(Silhouette Desire #1459)

**October: THE WILL TO LOVE**
(Silhouette Romance #1618)

**November: PROTECTING HIS OWN**
(Silhouette Intimate Moments #1185)

*Available at your favorite retail outlet*

*Where love comes alive™*

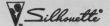

# SPECIAL EDITION™

Was it something in the water...
or something in the air?

Because bachelors in Bridgewater, Texas,
are becoming a vanishing breed—fast!

**Don't miss these three exciting stories of Texas
cowboys by favorite author Jodi O'Donnell:**

Deke Larrabie returns to discover
someone *else* he left behind....

## THE COME-BACK COWBOY
(Special Edition #1494)
September 2002

Connor Brody meets his match and gives her

## THE RANCHER'S PROMISE
(Silhouette Romance #1619)
October 2002

Griff Corbin learns about true
friendship and love when he falls for

## HIS BEST FRIEND'S BRIDE
(Silhouette Romance #1625)
November 2002

*Available at your favorite retail outlet.*

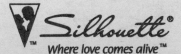

Where love comes alive™

**SILHOUETTE** *Romance*

# COMING NEXT MONTH

### #1618  THE WILL TO LOVE—Lindsay McKenna
*Morgan's Mercenaries: Ultimate Rescue*
With her community destroyed by an earthquake, Deputy Sheriff
Kerry Chelton turned to Sergeant Quinn Grayson to help establish order
and rebuild. But when Kerry was injured, Quinn began to realize that no
devastation compared to losing Kerry....

### #1619  THE RANCHER'S PROMISE—Jodi O'Donnell
*Bridgewater Bachelors*
Lara Dearborn's new boss was none other than Connor Brody—the
son of her sworn enemy! Connor had worked his entire life to escape
Mick Brody's legacy. But could he have a future with Lara when the
truth about their fathers came out?

### #1620  FOR THE TAKING—Lilian Darcy
*A Tale of the Sea*
Thalassa Morgan wanted to put the past behind her, something that Lou-
can—claimant of the Pacifica throne—wouldn't allow. Reluctantly she
returned to Pacifica as his wife to restore order to their kingdom. But
her sexy, uncompromising husband proved to be far more dangerous
than the nightmares haunting her....

### #1621  CROWNS AND A CRADLE—Valerie Parv
*The Carramer Legacy*
She thought she'd won a vacation to Carramer—but discovered her
true identity! Sarah McInnes's grandfather was Prince Henry Valmont—
and her one-year-old son the royal heir! Now, handsome, intense Prince
Josquin had to persuade her to stay—but were his motives political or
personal?

### #1622  THE BILLIONAIRE'S BARGAIN—Myrna Mackenzie
*The Wedding Auction*
What does a confirmed bachelor stuck caring for his eighteen-month-
old twin brothers do? Buy help from a woman auctioning her services
for charity! But beautiful April Pruitt was no ordinary nanny, and
Dylan Valentine wondered if his bachelorhood was the next item on
the block!

### #1623  THE SHERIFF'S 6-YEAR-OLD SECRET—Donna Clayton
*The Thunder Clan*
Nathan Thunder avoided intimate relationships—and discovering he had
an independent six-year-old daughter wasn't going to change that!
Gwen Fleming wanted to help her teenage brother. Could two mis-
matched families find true love?